Just Like Romeo & Juliet

D1488980

By:

Brooke St. James

3

So This is Love (Miami Stories #1)
All In (Miami Stories #2)
Something Precious (Miami Stories #3)

The Suite Life (The Family Stone #1)
Feels Like Forever (The Family Stone #2)
Treat You Better (The Family Stone #3)
The Sweetheart of Summer Street (The Family Stone #4)
Out of Nowhere (The Family Stone #5)

Delicate Balance (The Blair Brothers #1)
Cherished (The Blair Brothers #2)
The Whole Story (The Blair Brothers #3)
Dream Chaser (Blair Brothers #4)

Kiss & Tell (Novella) (Tanner Family #0)
Mischief & Mayhem (Tanner Family #1)
Reckless & Wild (Tanner Family #2)
Heart & Soul (Tanner Family #3)
Me & Mister Everything (Tanner Family #4)
Through & Through (Tanner Family #5)
Lost & Found (Tanner Family #6)
Sparks & Embers (Tanner Family #7)
Young & Wild (Tanner Family #8)

Easy Does It (Bank Street Stories #1)
The Trouble with Crushes (Bank Street Stories #2)
A King for Christmas (Novella) (A Bank Street Christmas)
Diamonds Are Forever (Bank Street Stories #3)
Secret Rooms and Stolen Kisses (Bank Street Stories #4)
Feels Like Home (Bank Street Stories #5)
Just Like Romeo and Juliet (Bank Street Stories #6)

Chapter 1

November 1995
Houston, TX

Anne Rose Kennedy

Everyone had things that stuck with them in life. I was still young, but I had lived through certain conversations and situations that were wedged into my memory so firmly I figured I'd never forget them.

For instance, Jason Hardesty was standing next to me at my kindergarten graduation when someone behind us passed out and fell forward, crashing into us. We almost fell off the stage. It was a heroic act by a parent in the first row that saved us. Several of us cried, and I was left with a sprained wrist.

Another memory that stuck out to me was the time Becky Gibson told me Santa wasn't real. In an unrelated conversation some years later, the same Becky also told me where babies came from.

I had no idea I was about to have one of those types of memorable conversations.

This news would turn out to be even bigger than Santa, but at the time, I thought I was meeting a woman about an article for the college newspaper.

I had talked to her assistant over the phone and he told me that since I was a senior, they were interested in having me write a short article about the UH Bachelor's in Nutrition program, which I was about to complete. I was not a writer, but the man on the phone assured me it was no big deal and that the editor just wanted to talk to me about it.

I walked into a Denny's, which was where she wanted to meet. Helen was the lady's name. I was supposed to meet her at 11am, and I walked into Denny's two minutes late. I normally liked to be early for things, but in Houston there was always traffic, and today it was particularly bad.

I was less nervous than I thought I would be about the meeting. I felt confident and, honestly, a bit like I would tell the lady I'd pass on doing it. I would have to see how our conversation went, but at this point, I didn't see myself as the *writing an article* type. As it stood, I rarely read them.

"I'm meeting a woman here," I said to the hostess. "Mrs. Elliot. Helen Elliot."

"Oh, yeah, I think it's that lady over there. Are you Anne?"

"Yes," I said, even though I went by Anne Rose, which was my first and middle name. Only people who didn't know me called me by my first name.

"I'll show you to her table," she said.

I followed the hostess through the restaurant.

I scanned my surroundings until I thought I spotted the right woman. There was a lady sitting alone at a table near the window. There were other people at other tables, but she was the only person I could see who was alone.

She was dressed in designer clothes and wearing a big hairdo. It was all teased and sprayed into an oversized helmet which she adjusted with a jewelry-adorned finger. There was a good amount of gold and diamonds on her hand and wrist. I knew she wasn't what I was expecting from an editor of a college newspaper, but I didn't give it much thought.

She stood when she saw me coming.

I smiled as I approached her.

She didn't smile much. She attempted one, but it was fleeting. She stared at me with an expression that I would call searching or appraising—something more intense than I expected. I held the smile and nodded at her as I came to stand behind my chair. I expected her to be the one to introduce herself, but all she said was, "Good God almighty, you are his spitting image."

"Hi, are you Helen Elliot?" I asked, blowing past her random comment.

"Oh, ye-yes, yes I am." She stared intently at me, looking confused, almost frazzled.

I reached out to shake her hand. "I'm Anne Rose Kennedy," I said. And when she still appeared to be lost in thought, I added, "I'm graduating from the Nutrition program at UH."

"Yes, yes, of course." She nodded absentmindedly as we took our seats. We got settled at the table.

I contemplated opening my silverware and putting my napkin on my lap, but she hadn't done the same, so I waited.

"Hello, can I get you something else to drink?" our waitress asked. She was looking at me as she came up to our table. She set two coffee cups in front of us. There were already two glasses of ice water sitting there.

"No ma'am, coffee's fine," I said.

"Okay, there's cream and sugar on the table, and I'll be right back with your apple pie."

She walked away, and the lady across from me, Helen, began shaking her head. "I don't know why she brought the coffee before the pie," she mumbled, looking dissatisfied.

She focused on me again as she added sugar to her coffee. I began adding cream and sugar to my own coffee, but I glanced at her frequently enough that I saw her staring at me. She gazed at me like she was thinking about something.

"Those green eyes," she said. She took a deep breath, staring without blinking. It took me a second to realize that her eyes were the same as mine.

"Yes, ma'am. You too, I see. I'm the only one in my family with them," I added, smiling and doing my best to keep the conversation light. I took a sip of my coffee, trying to be casual since she seemed to be a little on the intense side.

I saw the waitress approaching from the corner of my eye, and I glanced that way. "Oh, that was fast," I said, hoping the lady wouldn't give the waitress a hard time about the pie.

The waitress set the pies down, one in front of each of us. "Looks great, thank you," I said to her. The woman seemed to be a little socially awkward, and I didn't want her to be rude.

"This'll do, thank you," Helen said in a no-nonsense tone.

"Okay, I'll give you ladies a minute. Let me know if you need anything."

"Thank you," Helen said, rushing her along.

"I picked up a copy of the school newspaper after you called," I said. "You guys do a good job. I was surprised you didn't want to just meet on campus, though. I looked it up, and the newspaper office is in a building I pass every day on my way to class."

She cut into her pie with the side of her fork. I thought she was going to take a bite, but she didn't even lift it to her mouth. She looked up and stared at me, taking a deep breath. She was serious and thoughtful, like she was contemplating the meaning of life. I took a bite of my pie, chewing and thinking this was about the most awkward meeting I could ever imagine.

"I'm not sure what Gary Ryder told you," she said.

"Who's Gary Ryder?" I asked, confused.

"The man who called you and set up this meeting." Helen said.

She was serious and straight-faced.

My heart started beating faster because the guy who set up the meeting had told me his name was Rob Robertson. I realized, as I thought about it, that it was probably a made-up name. I looked around, wondering what was going on. I got a weird feeling from this lady.

"Did you not want to meet me to discuss writing an article?" I asked, poised to get up and walk out.

"No. I didn't even know that was what Gary told you. An article?"

I pushed my chair back and started to stand up.

"No, please, I beg you," she said in an urgent tone as she started to stand with me.

I stayed on the edge of my seat as I looked at her with a confused, defensive expression. "I think you have the wrong person," I said.

"No, I don't. Gary Ryder is a private investigator. He found you for me, and I know you're the right person. I see it."

I shook my head in confusion. "Listen, I don't know who you—"

"You're my granddaughter," she blurted out.

For a second, I wondered if there could possibly be any truth to what she was saying, but I quickly figured out there couldn't. She must have me confused with someone else. I shook my head regretfully at her. "I know all of my grandparents," I said. "I'm sorry, but you must have the wrong person." I used a tone of regret because she looked serious and desperate, like she was really hoping to find her granddaughter.

"Anne Kennedy," she said. She opened her eyes wide, staring at me, blinking at me in all seriousness with her eyes bulging out of her head. She leaned in closer with that intense expression.

"What are you doing?" I asked, leaning away.

"Look at my eyes," she said. "They're unmistakable. I passed them to my son, Michael, who passed them to you."

"I'm so sorry, ma'am, but my dad's name isn't Michael."

"It's Kyle Kennedy. And Janet is your mother. Your name is Anne, and you were born at Houston Methodist. You went to ICCS all twelve years of school, and now you go to college and work at the bookstore at the University of Houston."

"My name is Anne Rose," I said, calling her out on the one thing she got wrong. "Anne Rose. Not just Anne. Anyone who knows me would know that. I don't go by my first name. I never have." I felt shaken. It scared me that she knew so much.

I took in my surroundings. I knew this lady couldn't catch me if I got up and ran out, but who was to say that this *Gary Rider* character wasn't sitting in the parking lot waiting to ambush me.

I should have checked her credentials before I agreed to meet her. My heart was pounding, and I reminded myself to stay calm. I thought about excusing myself and going to the restroom where I could crawl out of the window like you see in the movies. I was imagining that play out, and for some reason, I imagined the window would be up high where I would have to stand on the sink to get to it.

In the time that I daydreamed my big escape, Mrs. Elliot (if that was really her name) pulled out a folder. She had already opened it by the time I started to excuse myself to go to the restroom. I was in the process of getting up, and I was about to tell her casually that I needed to use the restroom.

I touched my stomach, hoping that would make my abrupt departure more believable. She saw me leaving and she whipped out a photograph, turning it and flinging it in front of me. She did it so quickly that there was a paper rustling noise before it whacked on the table right next to the pie.

It was a large, 8x10 school picture of a boy who looked just like me. He had more masculine features, obviously, but there was an extremely strong resemblance—enough to make me stop in my tracks. I couldn't take my eyes off of it.

"This was my son in his senior year of high school," she said.

I figured as much since he was wearing a cap and gown. This man looked nothing like my dad, Kyle Kennedy, but he looked exactly like me. My father had dark brown eyes. My little sister did as well. I was the only one in my family with green eyes.

They matched the man in the picture, I had to give her that. In reality, it meant nothing, though. *Who was she to come in here with a picture of a man with green eyes and tell me I had been mistaken about my identity since birth?*

"If this man was my father, my mother would've already told me." I said as soon as the thought crossed my mind. My voice came out sounding shaky and I realized it was because I was staring at the picture and the unbelievable resemblance I shared with the man. My features were more rounded and delicate than his, but he looked like he could be my twin brother. I kept trying to look away, but I just couldn't take my eyes off of it for long. It wasn't just the color of his eyes. It was his wavy hair and the shape of his face. My eyes stung and I could feel tears beginning to form. I looked away, pushing the picture toward her.

"I know who my father is," I said. "And this could be a fake picture. How do I know that this guy even exists?"

"What in heaven's name... what in the world are you... just the fact that you think I'm making this up should tell you that you look just alike. You're Michael's daughter."

"I'm Kyle's daughter."

"Maybe by name. And maybe that's what your mother wants you to believe. Janet? Isn't that your mother's name?"

I stared at her, wondering whether or not there could be any truth to what she was saying.

I was stuck mentally. It was the equivalent of being speechless, only it was happening in my brain. I stared blankly at the table, absentmindedly taking in the picture and finding it hard to form a cohesive thought.

"I rarely speak to my own son," she said. "Michael. He was my only boy, and now I've been reduced to calling him on his birthday and Christmas. His father hasn't spoken to him in twenty years. We live in Galveston, and Michael caused me a lot of heartache when he lost his way and left home. He forced me to make a lot of enemies. There were wounds created that still haven't healed. He broke me down in the time before he left, and his father never forgave him for that."

"What does any of this have to do with me?" I asked.

"Our boy should've never moved to Houston. He should've stayed in Galveston. He could have worked for us and made a nice life for himself. He was ruined by a broken heart and then he ran off and made all sorts of mistakes."

She sounded disappointed and frustrated, and it only made me mad.

"Sooo, you called me to Denny's to tell me that you think you know who my real dad is, and that my existence is a big mistake?"

"Heavens no, my child, you are the only good thing that Michael did back then." She stared at me with tears welling in her eyes. "You don't know what my husband and I would give to have our son back. He's been lost to us for so many years that we don't know where to begin. I mean, our son knew about you all these years, and he just told me you existed. But I knew instantly I had to get to know you. I felt hope, like getting to know you would somehow be the same as me being able to go back and get things right with my son. I just know it. You're a fresh start for our family."

"N-no, ma'am, I'm not a fresh... I didn't come here expecting... I'm not going to... " I trailed off. I honestly didn't even know what to say to her. "If this is true, why wouldn't your son find me and tell me sooner?"

"Michael must be going through a midlife crisis. I don't know what's going on with him. I think he's dealing with a lot of his regret. My birthday was a couple weeks ago, and he called and told me I had a grandchild. I talked to him for a while, and one of the things he said was that you existed. He didn't even know if you were a boy or girl. He gave me your mother's name and told me briefly how they met, and Gary did the rest. He found you, got some information, and set up this meeting. I honestly can't believe it myself. I've been sitting here staring at you, and I still can't believe what I'm seeing. Anne Rose. What a beautiful name. You are the spitting image of my son, sweetheart. I just know you are his daughter, and I want you to know you have family who loves you and would love to get to know you."

I stared at her, trying to think of what in the world I could possibly say to all this. I felt shocked, stunned. I felt like my whole world had broken to pieces.

"You're saying all of this like it's no big deal, but you have to understand that it is a big deal to me. I'm not saying that I believe it's true. But even if it was, did it ever occur to you that maybe I *don't want to know*? My life is fine like it is. Maybe I don't want to know if my real dad is some other guy."

Chapter 2

"So, you're just picking up and going to Galveston to *meet* these people?" My best friend stared at me with a dumfounded expression like I had lost my mind.

"I'm thinking about it," I said. "Jennifer lives there. I could just tell my parents I'm going there for her. I don't even need to tell them anything. They'll just assume I'm busy or hanging out with you."

"Do you believe what that lady said?" she asked, still looking confused.

I shook my head. "I don't know. I didn't at first. She freaked me out a little. I almost got up and left the table. I thought she was kidnapping me or something."

"And now you're going to visit her in Galveston?"

"I think so," I said. "But it's not like I let her talk me into it easily. We sat there at Denny's and talked for two hours. She and her family own a restaurant over there, can you believe it? A big seafood restaurant! Like Red Lobster but better! She told me all about it."

I spoke in an amazed tone because I had *always* wanted to be a chef, and Maggie knew it. I would have gone to culinary school rather than college, but my parents told me that I wouldn't enjoy a life as a chef and that studying nutrition at the university would be the same thing, only more fulfilling.

At the time, I thought they might be right, but the longer I was in school the more I realized that I had settled for studying food and its nutritional value, which wasn't nearly as fun as cooking it.

My parents weren't trying to doom me to a bad life, but neither of them cared about food, and they didn't get the appeal of standing over a hot stove to prepare it. They didn't let me get in the kitchen much growing up. My mom had always cared more about keeping the house neat and tidy rather than cooking. We usually ate with my grandparents or got take out. Once a week or so, my mom would cook something, but it was always a dish with two or three ingredients, like spaghetti or hamburger helper. My dad ate eggs a lot, and he would cook those, but they honestly didn't care enough about eating food to keep quality ingredients in the house. There was a lot of ramen and frozen dinners.

I did more cooking at Maggie's house than at my own. I had a part-time job at the bookstore on campus, but I wasn't working enough to spend money on the types of food I wanted to cook.

"Now the truth comes out," she said. "You want to go over there so you can cook." Maggie smiled at me like she had me all figured out.

"No, no, it's not just that. I am curious about their restaurant, but who wouldn't be? Helen said it's a successful seafood restaurant, right on the water.

She said it's one of the most popular places in Galveston. Michael might inherit it one day with his sister, if he could ever get his life on track. Anyway, she said cooking was in my blood. Can you believe it? You know how I love to cook."

"Tons of people love to cook," Maggie said. "Most people love to cook."

"That's not true. And it's not the only reason I want to go over there. You should have seen that picture of her son. You wouldn't believe the resemblance. And she doesn't want anything from me," I added. "If she was asking me for something, or I got the impression that she was going to take advantage of me, I wouldn't even talk to her. But she doesn't want anything from me. She wants to give me stuff. She gave me a thousand dollars before we left Denny's."

"A *thousand dollars*?"

"Yes."

"And you took it?"

"Yes," I said.

"You're joking."

"I'm not joking."

"You didn't tell me she gave you money. A thousand dollars? Are you serious?"

"Yes," I said.

"Why are we not at the mall?"

I smiled and shrugged. "She said it was for missed birthdays and Christmases. I didn't want to take anything from her, but she insisted.

"A thousand dollars is a lot of money," Maggie said. "That might be sketchy."

"She's not sketchy. She's just an old lady who misses her son. There was a girl who drove him out of Galveston. She and her family. You know, relationship drama. Michael got devastated years ago and Mrs. Elliott never sees him. He hasn't talked to his dad in like twenty years."

"I don't know what to tell you," Maggie said shrugging. "It's both cool and freaky that she gave you a thousand bucks. What are you going to do with it?"

"I don't know," I said, "Maybe save it. I'll probably just save it."

"Does your mom know?"

"No way."

"You should tell her. Just ask your mom if she even knew a guy named Michael back then."

"No, Maggie. I'm not telling her. If what the lady said is true, then my mom kept it from me all these years."

"Well, then maybe it's not true," Maggie said.

"What if it is?" I asked.

She shrugged. "It seems like your mind is made up about going."

"It is," I said nodding. "I'm going down there, just for the day. Jennifer lives there now. I'll call her and go by to see her at her work so I don't have to lie to my mom."

"Are you talking about Jennifer from the BCM?" Maggie asked. We knew Jennifer Meyers from a student organization at UH. Maggie and I had only known each other since college, but we had become really close in the last few years. She was the one who had introduced me to Jennifer in the first place.

"Yeah," I said. "We told her we might come see her when she moved."

"Are you seriously going to connect with her when you go there, or are you just using her as an excuse?"

"I'm going to go by Jennifer's because I'm a terrible liar and if my mom starts questioning me about it, I want to have answers. That's another thing. I wanted to check with you and make sure I have the right number for Jennifer so I can call her."

"I think I have her home number, but you could always just call her work. She's full-time at that ballet studio. That's why she moved over there."

I smiled. "Yeah, that's what I was thinking. I knew I could reach her there. I remember her saying the name of the street it was on, so it shouldn't be too hard to find."

"Yeah, she did say the name of the street. What was it?"

"It's on Bank Street."

***

It was four days later, on a Friday, when I got in my car and headed down to Galveston.

I left at one o'clock and got to the island at two-thirty. I wanted to see the restaurant in its full glory on a Friday night, so I made plans to arrive that afternoon, eat dinner in the evening, and spend the night with Jennifer. As of now, I hadn't told Mrs. Elliot I was coming.

I went straight to the ballet studio because I knew that's where Jennifer would be. It was located in a gorgeous Victorian building. Everything was pretty in that downtown area near the Strand. I had been to Galveston a few other times, but we mostly stayed on the seawall, and I hadn't seen much else. The ballet studio was in a charming location.

I passed a diner on the same block, and I absentmindedly thought that I would get a cup of coffee there sometime during my trip.

I had all sorts of absent-minded thoughts about this cool little city. I found a parking spot near the ballet studio and walked inside feeling happy.

This day was completely on my terms.

Helen Elliott had no idea I was coming. I had no commitments and no plans to meet up with her. My only plan was to go to the restaurant and scope it out. I could go for some delicious seafood, and I had some extra money in my checking account, courtesy of Mrs. Elliot.

"Anne Rose Kennedy!" Jennifer was already calling my name as I walked into the door of the ballet studio. I smiled and waved in her general direction. She and two other female ballerinas were standing near each other. They looked like triplets. They were all dressed in practice ballet attire with their hair pulled back into neat buns. I had no problem finding my friend, though. She waved me over as they all continued to huddle around the window.

"You can't always see them from here," Jennifer said, making room for me at the window. "But right now you can."

"Boxers," one of the other girls said. "They're having a sparring session, and sometimes they... see? Look. They come right here by the window. That's Will right there," she added. "His dad owns that gym. And the other guy, that's Tara's husband."

Jennifer looked at me. "Tara's our boss," she explained.

We all stayed glued to the window as we watched the two gentlemen spar, shifting and weaving and trying to hit each other. The gym wasn't directly across the street, so we had to crane our necks to watch, but it was amazing to see them move around and exchange controlled, technical blows. They were both handsome young men, and I didn't know much about boxing, but it looked like they knew what they were doing.

"Will comes over here by the window because he *knows* we watch him." the first girl said.

"He only knows we watch him because you told him," Jennifer said. "He can't see us with these windows."

We all continued to spy for another minute or so until the two guys finished the round and walked away from the window. All of the ballerinas looked around smiling like they were noticing me for the first time.

"I'm Candice," the talkative one said.

"Emily," the other one added shyly.

"This is my friend, Anne Rose," Jennifer said, introducing me as we all started to walk away from the window. "We went to college together. You were a year or two behind me, right?"

"Yeah, I'm not quite done," I said. "One semester to go."

"Oh, wow, that went by quick," she said. "It feels like I just graduated."

The three of them began to stretch.

"So, is that boxer your boyfriend or something?" I asked, trying to make conversation. I was looking in Candice's general direction since she was the most vocal, but she shook her head.

"I *wish*," she said, rolling her eyes. "Emily dated him and so did Jennifer, but I went to school with him, and he just doesn't see me that way."

"I wouldn't call what we did *dating*," Jennifer said. "I'd call it hanging out. Nobody dates Will. He's a player. He's a butterfly boy."

I thought of the manly guy I saw in the window and made a face of confusion at her for calling him that.

"As in, he's just in it for the butterflies," she clarified. "He doesn't even *date* anyone. He just flirts with you, and kisses you, and gives you all sorts of butterflies, and then out of nowhere, he goes back to being your friend."

"Everybody loves Will," Candice said. "Don't let them fool you, he's a good guy. I actually wish I was one of the girls he flirted with and kissed and then left alone. I'd rather that than being invisible to him."

"You're not invisible to him. He talks to you all the time."

"Yeah, but I'm not visible in the way I want to be," Candice said.

"Shhhhh," Jennifer said. "I hear Tara coming out of her hole."

I cut my eyes at Jennifer, wondering if I should be scared.

"She's cool," she explained. "Will is her brother. Their dad owns that boxing gym. Their family basically owns this block. Tara and her husband live upstairs. His name's Trey. He was the one boxing with Will just now."

I just shook my head and shrugged innocently since I didn't know any of these people.

Chapter 3

Just then, another ballerina came from the hallway, smiling at me as she crossed the room.

"This is the owner of our studio, Tara Castro," Jennifer said. "This is my friend, Anne Rose. She's visiting from Houston."

"Anne Rose, that's a cool name," Tara said. "Is it your first name?"

"First and middle," I said.

"I like that," she said, nodding. "I used to know a girl named Anna Kate."

"That's a good one," I said, nodding.

"She likes weird names," Jennifer said. "Her son's name is Nickel."

"That's a nickname," Tara said.

(I wanted to make the corny, impromptu joke that it was a Nickel-name and not just a nickname, but I kept it to myself.)

"My husband is William, but we call him Trey," Tara continued. "We named Nick William after his dad, but I have Williams all over the place on my side, too. My dad is William and my brother. Our son is the fifth William in our immediate family, so we call him Nick or Nickel for five."

"Speaking of your brother, we saw Will and Trey fighting each other just now," Candice said. She was still close enough to the front of the studio that she was able to see out to Bank Street. "They're doing it again," she said, causing Jennifer to walk that way to catch a glimpse.

"Tara's dad is a famous boxer," Candice said. "Do you remember Marvin Jones?"

Of course I knew Marvin Jones. He was an old boxer—the most famous old-timey boxer I could think of. I had seen footage of him in black and white.

"Marvin Jones is your dad?" I asked, a little stunned and wondering how old he had to be when he had her.

Tara laughed. "No, but he may as well be my grandpa," she said. "He's like family. He's my dad's coach. My dad bought the gym from him, but Marvin still works there and lives upstairs and everything. He's in his late seventies, I think."

"Her dad is famous, too," Candice said. "Easy Billy Castro. He's a boxer."

"I know exactly who that is," I said, feeling amazed and taking a step back. That guy was super famous. My dad didn't even watch boxing, and he had talked about Easy Billy. "That's crazy that Marvin Jones and Easy Billy Castro are at the same place," I said.

"Coach Jones is the one who discovered my dad," Tara said. "He's like a father to him."

"That is so cool," I said. "I know of both of those guys, but I had no idea they knew each other."

Tara laughed, getting a kick out of my statement.

"Is your brother going to be famous like your dad?" I asked, since she was standing there, smiling at me.

"Not for boxing," she said. "He's taken a couple of amateur matches, but it was just for the experience. He likes training, but if he was interested in taking it all the way, like my dad, he'd be training full-time instead of working.

"Oh, so he has a job?" I asked.

"Yeah. Right next door at my uncle's hardware store."

I smiled inwardly, remembering the comment about her family owning this whole block. I liked Tara instantly. She had a nice smile and she looked me in the eyes like she was genuinely engaged in the conversation.

"How long are you in town?" Tara asked as she went to the bar and began to stretch.

"Just till tomorrow," I said, moving to the side of the room. "I've always wanted to check out Galveston. Are you sure you don't mind if I crash on your couch tonight?" I asked Jennifer.

They looked like they were about to start class, so I figured I would need to be going soon.

"Our couch," Emily said.

"More like Tara's couch," Candice added.

Jennifer smiled at me. "Tara's my boss and my landlord. Technically the couch is hers. Emily's my roommate, so the couch is hers, too... but, no, none of us mind if you sleep on it."

All of us laughed at her statement.

"Okay, well, I wrote down the address," I said. "And I have a map. I'll plan on being there by nine or so, if that's not too late."

"No, no problem. Just call me if something comes up and your plans change. We have another roommate, but she's not home half the time."

I heard the door open, and turned to find some young ballerinas walking in. "I'll let you guys go," I said, starting to walk away.

"You don't have to, those are Miss Candice's girls," Tara said.

Emily and Candice had taken off toward the door to greet the girls.

"They teach the four o'clock beginner class," Tara said. "They're going to the back room."

She smiled at me as she got into another stretching position. I thought it was nice that she wasn't in a hurry for me to leave. Watching her stretch made me want to do the same. If I didn't have on jeans, I would have asked if I could go out there and stretch with them.

"Are you traveling alone?" Tara asked.

"I am," I said. "I've just always wanted to come to Galveston."

"What are you going to do while you're here? Go to the beach? It's pretty warm today, for November."

"I was planning on going there," I said, nodding. "And then I'd like to get some good seafood tonight. I was thinking about going to a place called Elliot's."

"Oh, no, you don't want to eat there," Tara said.

"Have you been there before?" she asked.

"No, I haven't. I just heard it was good."

She shrugged. "I don't like it. If I was going to eat seafood, I'd definitely go to Miller's."

"Oh, okay, thank you," I said, smiling even though it was disappointing to hear her say such things about the restaurant.

I had imagined that going a lot differently. I had hoped to hear people say it was the best restaurant in town.

"It's wherever you want to eat, though," Tara said. "Carson's Diner on the corner has really good food, too." She smiled. "And there's all sorts of junk food at the boardwalk."

"I have a hard time resisting junk food," I admitted, smiling and touching my stomach. I turned toward the door because I knew it was about to open. I could see students coming in—a group from the sidewalk and others from a school bus that had just stopped right out front.

"Whoa," I said.

"Yeah, it's the after-school rush," Jennifer said. "It's quiet time right now, though. They work on homework or sit and stretch until we get started."

"Okay, well, I'm going to get out of your way," I said. "It was nice meeting you, Tara, and good seeing you, Jennifer. Thank you for letting me crash at your place."

"Oh, it's no problem," Jennifer said. "I might hang out with some friends tonight. You're welcome to come with us. I thought you would until you mentioned getting home at nine. We'll probably head out at around eight o'clock. If I leave before you get home, I'll leave the door unlocked for you. Emily might be home, but if she's not, I'll make sure the door's open."

"Thank you," I said, waving at them.

There were girls coming in as I was going out, and after a few seconds of smiling and scooting past young ballerinas and their mothers, I found myself on the sidewalk.

It should not have put me in a bad mood for Tara to say that she didn't like Helen Elliot's restaurant, but I couldn't stop thinking about it. I didn't even know for sure that I was related to this woman, but I still didn't want people disliking her restaurant. I spaced out and thought about it as I stood on the sidewalk for a moment.

I realized that I couldn't just stand there forever, so I started walking toward the diner down the street. I figured a cup of afternoon coffee might help me focus.

I walked in front of the hardware store, and as I walked, I glanced toward the boxing gym which was across the street. I could see more of the room from this angle. There were what must have been thirty people in the room. It was a larger place than I expected, so I couldn't even see all the way inside.

I only gazed into the window for a few seconds before forcing myself to look away. Bank Street Boxing. I read the sign above the door before glancing at a group of people walking down the sidewalk in front of the gym.

I stared all around, at the buildings and stores and all the different people inside and on the streets. Galveston was a neat little city. It was hard to believe that this was so close to Houston. It felt like I was in a completely different country, or maybe a different era. There were modern cars around, but it didn't feel like the nineties. This place felt stuck in older times—in a good way.

I focused on the diner, which only confirmed what I was thinking. There was a ton of chrome and black and white, and it looked like it had been on that corner since the fifties. I waited till I got to the corner to cross the street.

Galveston was a gorgeous city, and I had a place to rest my head tonight. I should have been having a grand old time. But I hated that Jennifer's boss had bad things to say about the Elliot's restaurant. It was sad, but that had really stuck with me.

I decided I would ask someone else about it, hoping to get a better response. There was a group of people walking down the sidewalk, headed my way, and because it was at the forefront of my mind, I said something right then.

"Excuse me, may I ask you guys something?"

It was a family, parents with three adolescent children, the oldest one was a teenager and the other two were ten or twelve.

"Of course," the woman said, being friendly.

"I'm just visiting town, and I was going to eat some food at Elliot's seafood restaurant tonight. Do you know if that place is any good?"

"Oh, uh, sorry but we're actually from out of town, too," the lady said, looking regretful.

"Yeah, but that was one of the restaurants the lady at Moody Gardens recommended," the man said.

"Oh, was it, really?" she asked. "Oh well, if it was one she mentioned, then I'm sure it's good," she said, smiling at me.

"Oh great, thank you!" I said, smiling and feeling much better now that I got the answer I was looking for.

They continued walking down the sidewalk, headed the way I had just come, while I crossed the street to get to the diner.

I liked going to diners like this. I had been raised eating out, so I had been in plenty of them. There was a similar one close to campus, and I went there quite a bit for a cup of coffee.

At home, I usually went to restaurants with someone else, but that wasn't an option here. I didn't mind, though. If I wanted to have someone with me today I would've asked Maggie. I wanted to be alone on this trip.

I went into the diner, smiling and feeling relieved when I saw that there were several open barstools at the counter.

My mom always liked to sit at the bar at places like this. I had watched her make conversations with waitresses and cooks dozens of times in my childhood.

"Sit anywhere you like," the lady said to me.

I took a seat on a stool close to the end with one seat separating myself and the guy on my left. He was an older man. There was a group of people on the other side of him, but I couldn't tell if they were together. It didn't matter. I figured with the empty barstool as a buffer I would barely talk to him, anyway.

Chapter 4

It was a good thing my trip to the diner didn't work out as planned. I talked to that older gentleman at the bar for what must have been an hour. He was about to leave when I came in, but we hit it off, and one topic led to another, so he wound up sitting there to talk to me.

Mitchell was his name, and we had just finished our conversation and decided to say goodbye. I was also ready to leave, but I let him head out before me so we didn't have to walk out together. I was all smiles because of our conversation, though.

I thought back to it as I sat there looking into my purse to waste some time. I had already left a tip, but I dug in my wallet to get an extra dollar to add to it. Mitchell had told me quite a bit about Elliot's restaurant. He was really familiar with it and said it was a Galveston tradition. We talked about other things, too, but the restaurant was a big part of our conversation. I smiled at myself when I thought back to how much I wanted to talk about that restaurant. Mitchell must've thought I was really hungry for seafood.

He had been gone for a minute now, so I began to get situated to leave.

"You must be thinking about something funny," I heard a man say from behind me.

I turned. It was the guy from the boxing gym. Will. Or so I thought it was. He had dark brown hair and eyes. I could see the resemblance to Jennifer's boss, Tara, now that he was close to me. It was either her brother or her husband, but I assumed it was her brother.

"Why would you say that?" I asked. "Did you ask if I thought something was funny?"

I wondered if he had even been the one to say it. I assumed he had. He was standing right beside me. He was situated higher than me since I was still seated, and I stared at him, trying not to notice his stature or his face, which was too handsome for words. I was taken aback by how nice-looking he was. He had big brown eyes with straight masculine features, and his face had perfect symmetry. It was no wonder Candice had seemed so desperate about him. I really hoped this wasn't Tara's husband I was swooning over, but I knew it couldn't be. He looked too much like her. I had been impressed through the window, but this guy was even better up close. He was big and athletic, and he wore an easy, approachable grin. I could see why Jennifer's friends were crazy about him.

"Because you were smiling," the guy said.

"Yeah, but you came up from behind me."

"There's a mirror," he said, pointing behind the counter. "And you were smiling a minute ago, too. I could see you from the sidewalk."

"Oh, uh, I was just thinking. I met a nice person and we had a good conversation just now, so I was just smiling."

"Who'd you meet?" he asked, sitting right next to me as if I had asked him to. He didn't know that I knew his sister, so I wasn't expecting him to sit by me. Even Mitchell had been a stool away. I shifted, feeling surprised that he was now so close.

"What?"

"Who was the person you had a conversation with? Who made you smile?"

"His name was Mitchell. He was just a random man—a nice man."

"My name is Will," he said, smiling and extending his hand for me to shake. "I'm a random nice man, too."

He was charming. He was nice and he was confident and humble in equal portions. I honestly hated to leave

"I was just leaving," I said, since I had my purse in my hand and was about to stand up.

He looked injured. "Did I say something wrong?"

"No, but you just got here, and I was leaving, so I was just saying... I didn't want you to take it personal when I got up."

"So, I guess it's out of the question for you to stay."

"I wouldn't say it's out of the question, but I was about to stand up when you walked up."

"Well, that's okay. It doesn't mean you can't stay and talk for another minute."

I smiled. He was so irresistible that it actually made me happy that he wanted me to stay. "What do you want to talk about?" I asked, pretending to be nonchalant.

"You," he said. "Who are you? What's your name?"

"I am a college student, a senior. I live in Houston. I'm here in Galveston for one day. My name is Anne Rose Kennedy, and I think I might have met your sister."

"Hello, Anne Rose Kennedy," he said, staring at me as he tried out my name. "I'm Will. How did you meet my sister?"

"That's it?"

"What's it?" he asked.

"I gave you way more than my name," I said.

He smiled. "You said you knew my sister, so I thought you knew something about me already. You want more? I ate oatmeal for breakfast. And eggs. I have my own apartment, and I still stop by my parents' a lot of the time because my dad makes breakfast."

"Your dad?" I asked, sounding surprised. I had already been told that Easy Billy Castro was his father. I had seen footage of the man in boxing matches so it surprised me to think of him cooking breakfast. "I met your sister today. Your sister is Tara, right?"

"Yeah, where'd you meet her?"

"At her studio. They were telling me about y'all's dad, and I knew he was a famous boxer, so I didn't picture him making breakfast."

"Oh, my dad does most of the cooking at the house. He loves to cook. What were you doing in my sister's studio?"

"My friend, Jennifer, works there. I was just over there a little while ago. I met your sister, and they pointed to your dad's gym and told me who you were."

"So, are you a ballerina?"

"No. I just know Jennifer from college."

"What'd you study in college?" he asked.

"Ballet," I said.

My face broke into a grin, letting him know I was joking, and he laughed like I got him for a second.

"Nutrition," I added.

He smiled and shook his head. "Why nutrition?" he asked thoughtfully. "What kind of job do you want to do with that?"

"I don't know yet," I said. "I think I can get a pretty good job as a dietitian somewhere. I honestly haven't looked into it. Mostly because it's not really what I want to do. I only got into nutrition because I wanted to be a chef."

"Why don't you just quit and go to school to be a chef instead?"

I had to smile at that. "I wanted to, but my parents talked me out of it. And I'm sure they're right. My dad worked in a restaurant for a few years during college. He was a waiter, but he said that the hours are terrible and the chefs complained about it all the time. I just can't make that work and raise a family."

"Oh, I didn't know you had a family," he said, pulling back a little.

"I don't. Not yet. But one day. You know, I'll be glad I don't have to stay out till all hours of the night, cooking for other people." I felt like my father when that sentence came out of my mouth.

"But wouldn't you rather spend bad hours doing something you love than good hours doing something you hate?"

I stared at him, blinking. I let out a little breath since I was somewhat speechless for a second. "Maybe you're right," I said. "Maybe I should have insisted that my family let me follow that dream. I think they would have supported me if I had been more disagreeable about it. But I only have one semester to go now, so I'm sort of stuck." I shrugged and smiled a little. "And I can learn to cook when I get a better job and pay for my groceries," I said with a shrug.

Will turned as my waitress came by. "Hey Ms. Diane, I'll have a cup of coffee, and two chocolate chip cookies, please." She nodded, and Will focused on me again. "Do you know how to cook at all?" he asked, seeming genuinely curious.

"I know a little. I do some cooking when I can. But I only know about one percent of what I want to know. I need way more practice, for sure. I still mess up." I smiled at him. "I do love it, though, and I think I could be really good at it with more practice."

"I guess if you're not going to go to school to be a chef, nutrition is sort of the next best thing."

"Yeah, it does carry over a little bit," I said nodding. "I did learn some things I'll take with me."

He let out a little laugh. "I should hope so, after four years of education," he said.

"Did you go to college?"

"I did. I studied business and marketing. I work for my uncle and I thought it would be the best thing to help me do the job."

I nodded, looking at him and smiling. "I thought you were going to tell me you were a boxing coach with all that zigging and zagging you were doing earlier."

"You saw me boxing?" he asked.

"I saw a little," I admitted.

"What were you doing checking me out? I thought you had a family on the way."

I pulled back, furrowing my eyebrows at him. "First, I'm not checking you out. I was just, I just thought it was cool watching *anyone* box. Tara's husband looked cool, too. It's a cool sport. And second, I don't have a family on the way."

41

"I thought that was what you said," he said.

"No."

"So, you're single, but you're *not* checking me out," he clarified.

"Yes," I said calmly, even though I didn't quite mean it. I was checking him out. Will Castro was irresistible. My heart had been pounding since I turned and saw him standing there.

"Well, that's great," he said, smiling.

"What's great?" I asked.

"You being single was the hard part. Getting you to check me out is easier than getting you to be single."

I wanted to say something to deny him, to tell him he was too confident, that he was saying too much to someone he just met, but I couldn't. Will was impossible to resist. He was sweet and I wanted to *at least* be friends with him. I wanted more than that. I was happy that he seemed interested in me. I was interested in him. Goodness. I normally wasn't this distracted by handsome men.

Diane put his coffee and cookies in front of him, and the distraction made me realize how mesmerized I was. I turned to leave, only because I knew I should before I got myself in trouble with this guy. I was headed out when he came in, and if I stayed much longer it would be obvious that I was interested.

"Why would you leave now? Our cookies just got here," he said.

I hesitated on the edge of my stool, turning around to look at him. I didn't slouch at all around Will. I had to smile at myself when I realized I was sitting so straight.

"I thought those were for you," I said.

"One's yours," he said. "When a man is sitting next to a woman and he orders two cookies, one of them is obviously for her."

"Oh, is that how it works?"

He was being funny, and I shook my head at him and smiled.

"Yes," he said, pushing the plate towards me. "Don't you know diner etiquette?"

"Oh, okay, if it's a matter of etiquette... " I said as I relaxed onto my stool. I reached out and took a cookie. "Thank you," I added just before I took a bite.

I looked at Will as I chewed.

"You're welcome," he said. He also took a bite of his cookie. We chewed for a moment in silence, glancing at each other, checking each other out in an almost comical way as we ate our cookies.

"Mmm, these are really good," I said.

"I know."

"I'll bet you're hungry after all that working out next door. Do you want half of mine? I can break off the part I didn't touch."

"I don't care if you touched it," he said.

"Oh, but you do want some?" I asked, moving to break the cookie.

"No, no, I don't want any, but if I did want some, I wouldn't care if you touched it. I would want you to touch it."

He looked me right in the eyes, and his boldness made me feel warm inside. I tucked my hair behind my ear.

"I like your green eyes," he said.

I took another bite of the cookie as a distraction.

"I like your brown eyes," I said.

I tried to seem casual, but we were definitely flirting, and I felt myself blush as the words came out of my mouth. I took the last sip of coffee out of the cup that was, thank goodness, still in front of me.

"I just took a shower," he said. "I don't always shower when I finish class, but today I did."

I laughed at how random Will's statement was. I was constantly smiling because he was fun and easy to be around. "Okay, thank you. I appreciate the good hygiene."

I liked talking to Will. Just his presence and demeanor made me smile.

"Hey, there's a birthday thing tonight," he said. "My Aunt Laney has a birthday today, and so do her two twins—they're both about my age, Jenny and Josh. Plus, two other peoples' birthdays are in the next couple of weeks. So, a bunch of us are getting together to celebrate tonight. My Aunt Abby, a different aunt, is having us all over to her house. I was thinking you might want to go by there with me."

Chapter 5

I came extremely close to accompanying Will Castro to his family birthday celebration. He was the most fascinating guy I had ever met, and I almost made the mistake of getting swept off of my feet by him that afternoon. It was insanely difficult for me to turn down his invitation, but I knew I had to stay on track.

For one, I had plans to check out the restaurant. I felt compelled to dig deeper into the information Helen Elliot had given me. I needed to know if Michael Elliot was my father, and I wanted to see what this family was all about.

Plus, Will was a butterfly boy, like Jennifer had said. Believe me, the butterflies were real and they were wonderful, and I would have loved to give in to them, but I knew I couldn't. That sort of excitement was temporary, and this information about the Elliots, well, it could be life-changing.

I loved meeting Will, and I told him so, but I regretfully declined his invitation to the birthday party. We did sit in that diner and talk for a while, though. I stayed with Will even longer than I did with Mister Mitchell. I didn't mean to stay there so long, but our conversation flowed, and time flew because we were having fun. We exchanged phone numbers, but I was almost certain we wouldn't use them—especially after what Jennifer had told me.

By the time I left Carson's Diner, it was almost dinner time. I went straight to the Elliot's restaurant, which was easy to find. It was even grander than I expected, and I knew I would have a hard time working up the nerve to walk in there. I meandered on the beach for a while, thinking about everything and trying to pump myself up to go inside. I wondered if it was true that Michael Elliott was my father. If so, then my mother obviously knew it. And she was either lying to my father, or he knew and they were both lying to me.

I had already gone through all types of scenarios and feelings, but new thoughts kept coming up as I walked on the beach. I was haunted by emotion, doubt, and insecurity. And then I thought of Will, and I had to smile. I remembered specific exchanges we had at the diner. He was easy to be around, and I smiled thinking it must be a family trait since his father's nickname was Easy.

My encounter with Will Castro turned out to be a blessing. Thinking of him and the random fun I had with him was what gave me the distraction I needed to work up the nerve to go into that restaurant.

It had gotten busier there since I first arrived, so I decided to go in before all the tables filled up. There was a huge deck outside with plants and palm trees and a lot of wood décor. As I approached, I realized that it felt a bit like I was getting onto a ship. I liked this place, and I couldn't help but grin in spite of my raging nerves.

It was already busy in there. I could see that a lot of the tables were full, and there were a few people in the lobby. Two young women were at the hostess stand, along with an older gentleman. I instantly assumed the man must be Helen's husband. This would mean he must be my biological grandfather. I reminded myself that I didn't even know if any of this was true.

"Welcome to Elliot's!" the man said with a sweet old-man smile.

"How many tonight?" one of the girls asked.

"Oh, uh, it's just me. One, please."

"Oh, okay," she said. "You're welcome to sit at the bar, or I could get you a table."

"I'll take a table, please," I said, since I wanted to look out and see the atmosphere in the restaurant and not the bar.

"I'll take her," the old man said. He leaned in and grabbed a menu from the hostess stand.

"Oh, uh, are you sure?" the girl asked, sounding surprised.

"Yes, I am," he said, simply.

"W-well, yes sir, twenty-six is open," she said.

"Twenty-six it is," the man said with a smile. He stepped forward and put his arm out for me, wanting me to grab it, telling me he was about to escort me to a table.

My heart pounded and I felt like I wanted to cry.

"Are you sure, with your hip, Mister Elliot?" the other girl asked.

"I'll make it," he said. "It'll be my physical therapy for the day."

I took his arm since he was still offering it to me and I didn't want to leave him hanging. We took off walking together. I felt a resemblance to him. He had dark eyes, unlike mine, but he had a square head and jaw and a thick sturdiness to his frame that reminded me of my own. I tried to remind myself not to get carried away in making comparisons, but it was impossible not to.

"I had a hip replacement two months ago, and they're still babying me about it." He paused, so I glanced at him, and he winked. "I'm just teasing. I like them to baby me. I'm still not quite right from it," he said, with a deprecating smile as we slowly walked through the restaurant.

"Two months isn't that long," I said. "I can understand why you're not quite right. It'll probably take a while."

He was doing his best not to limp, but it took effort. We glanced at each other as we walked slowly. He smiled at me when our eyes met, and I felt, based on his facial expression, that he knew who I was. Because of this, I got nervous and began speaking again.

"It smells delicious in here, and it's a really nice restaurant," I said. "I'm excited to try your food."

"Thank you, sweetheart. Is it your first time joining us for dinner?"

"Yes, sir."

"Well, welcome," he said. "I'm Mike Elliot, the owner. We're famous for our blackened redfish and our crawfish enchiladas. Either of those are really popular."

I made a mental note to order both of them. I followed him to a gorgeous table for two overlooking the water.

"This one's better than twenty-six," he said, setting the menu and silverware on the table. "I'll put you here instead." I started to sit down, but I stopped when he put a hand on my arm. "Stop," he said. "Before you sit down, I'd like to..." He trailed off, staring straight at me. "I believe my wife had some pictures of you on our dining room table." He spoke slowly and thoughtfully, and I was scared, but I responded as calmly as I could.

"Yes, sir."

"Have you ever met my wife, Helen Elliot?"

"Yes, sir," I said, staring at him and feeling like I could barely get the words out.

His grip tightened on my arm. I had no idea what he was thinking.

I cleared my throat and took a deep breath. "Miss Helen doesn't know I came here tonight," I said. "Nor do my parents. I just came to eat some dinner, if you don't mind."

"Would you mind if I join you?"

"No sir, not at all." (Because what else was I going to say?)

He got the attention of a nearby server, and told him to get word to the hostesses that he would be having dinner at table sixteen.

Mike Elliot ordered two appetizers and three entrees, and we sat and ate until we were about to pop. We connected over food. We never talked about me being his granddaughter. Things never got awkward. We ordered food, we ate food, and we talked about food.

He was a chef, and I must have asked him four hundred questions about cooking. It was so much fun that I wasn't even aware of the busy restaurant around us until he would mention something in the restaurant and bring my attention to it.

All of the dishes were delicious, and I asked him question after question about how they were made. He took pleasure in talking to me about it.

We ate dessert, and then we sat and talked for another hour over coffee. It was after 8pm when we left our table. Mister Elliot would not even consider letting me pay. He took me to the kitchen, and we watched the chefs and runners work while he explained what was going on. It had slowed down considerably in the restaurant, but there was still a lot going on, and I loved watching the action.

He told me so many things that there was no way I would remember it all. I tried to take it in, though, because I just loved being around a kitchen. I peeked over the chef's shoulder. I watched in awe as the simmering skillet caused the scallops to turn white with perfectly crisp brown edges. I was smitten.

I had no idea how Jennifer's boss could ever say that this place didn't have good food. Everyone seemed to be paying attention to detail. Maybe they were on their best behavior since the boss was around. If so, they had me fooled. It was amazing. It was one of the nicest restaurants I had ever been to, and the kitchen was wonderful.

After spending a while in the kitchen, Mister Elliot and I headed toward the hostess stand. "We're slowing down," he said, stopping to adjust some things on a nearby unoccupied table.

"Who do you have with you, Mister Elliot?" a lady said from behind us.

I turned to find a woman with a round face and dimples, smiling at me. I assumed she was a customer.

"Deann, this is Anne Rose," he said.

She wore a smile as she scanned my appearance. "Well, you know who she looks like..." she said, shaking her head and peering at me.

"Who?" he said.

"Y'all. She looks like part of your family. That's an Elliot if I've ever seen one."

"I know, I thought the same thing," he said, laughing and nodding. "Anne Rose Kennedy," he said. "She's interested in becoming a chef."

"Oh, well, isn't that lovely?" the woman said. "Mike Elliot is just the man to talk to about that. He's been feeding our family just about every Friday night for twenty years. We have all of our special occasions here, too. And they do catering."

"It's a beautiful restaurant," I agreed.

Mike checked on her to make sure they had a good experience that night, and then we told her goodbye.

He and I continued walking to the front of the restaurant.

"Back in the day, I stayed till closing every night," he said. "But nowadays, I'm usually at home by eight-thirty. Helen will be calling if I stay much longer."

"Oh, I'm sorry, you should go."

He stopped walking when I said that, and he turned to hug me. It was the first time he had done anything like that, and I went into the hug even though it was a little stiff.

"Don't ever apologize," he said, patting me on the back. "You have no idea how much I enjoyed spending time with you."

"Thank you, me too," I said. And I meant it.

"I'd love to give you some knives and an apron if you'll come see me again sometime."

"What's that mean? To cook?" I asked, trying not to seem excited.

"Yes, to cook," he said smiling. "I'll teach you everything I know."

My heart began racing. It was like winning the lottery and also feeling like you couldn't accept the prize.

"I'll, uh, I'm, that's so nice of you. Are you serious?"

"Yes, I am. Come back tomorrow, and I'll start showing you some things. Saturday mornings are good for me."

"Oh, my goodness, that's so tempting," I said.

"Come then," he said, staring at me sincerely.

"If not tomorrow, but another Saturday, if I decide to come back and take you up on that offer... would it be okay for me to just call up here at the restaurant and ask for you?"

"Sure. I'm here a lot of the time. But didn't Helen give you our home number?"

"Yes sir."

"Please, sweetheart, give us a call. We'd love to see you again. And I'm serious about teaching you how to cook. I can tell you're a nautral."

I smiled and nodded like I was excited. Because part of me was. But part of me was disappointed, too. I didn't have the heart to tell him that this was just a field trip from my regular life and that coming here more often and being a chef wasn't part of the plan. It was a little heartbreaking, but I knew there was a distinct possibility that I would never see any of these people again. I pondered these things as we made our way to the front door.

I thought of my whole afternoon in Galveston. I thought of Jennifer, Tara, Candice, Emily, the diner... Mitchell, and then Will. *Goodness, had it been today that I met Will Castro?* My unexpected evening with Mister Elliot had briefly pushed Will out of my mind. But now that I was leaving the restaurant, thoughts of Will flooded in. I wondered if he was finished with his family's birthday party.

I was ecstatic with how my evening had played out, but I thought of Will and wondered what would have happened if I had accepted his invitation. I was thinking mostly about Will as I walked to the parking lot with Mike Elliot. I knew our evening was over, and now my mind was free to think of other things.

Mike hugged me again when we parted ways, and it meant something to me because I could tell he wasn't the hugging type. He was friendly and he often touched a shoulder, but I could tell it was a stretch for him to ask for a hug.

I smiled as I drove to Jennifer's house. I knew I might never see Will Castro or Mike Elliot again, but each of them, for different reasons, had made my evening absolutely unforgettable.

Chapter 6

Will Castro
The following morning

"Hello?" Jennifer picked up the phone sleepily the following morning. She glanced at the little white box on the nightstand, and saw Will's number on her caller ID.

It was 8am on a Saturday, which was an odd time for him to call.

"Jennifer?" Will said when she picked up.

"Yeah."

"Were you sleeping?"

She cleared her throat. "Yeah."

"Is... I'm sorry to wake you up. I was just wondering if Anne Rose was still at your house. I'm on my way to work, and I was going to come by there and try to talk to her before she left."

Will paused. There was silence.

"Hello?" he asked.

"W-uh-I didn't know. I don't know. I just woke up. I can barely even..." Jennifer's voice was muffled and she cleared her throat again. "Um, what?"

"Anne Rose," he said. "Your friend from Houston. She said she was spending the night with you."

"Yeah, she did."

"I was making sure she was still there. I was going to come by your house."

"Right now?" she asked, sounding groggy and annoyed.

"I know she was planning on leaving early," Will said.

He felt desperate to see her. He couldn't get her off of his mind. She had a real personality. He felt like they had connected in a way he didn't usually connect with women. She had these cat-like green eyes that seemed to stare right into his heart and cut through all the pretense. The memory of those eyes still haunted Will. He had to see her again. He had to check and see if she was as wonderful as he remembered.

"Just come over then, I guess," Jennifer moaned, still annoyed. "I'm not gonna stop you."

"Is she there? I'd like to tell her I'm coming."

"Uhhhhh!" Jennifer let out a loud, frustrated groan causing Will to pull the phone from his ear. "She's way out there in the living room," she said.

But Will could hear her moving and he knew she was getting out of the bed, even as she complained. Jennifer was quiet on the phone. Will could hear the sound of her footsteps. She let out another frustrated groan.

"Uhhhh, she's not out here. Look. She left a note."

Again, Jennifer got quiet.

"Jennifer?" Will asked, after a minute.

"I was reading the note. She said 'thanks' and all that, but she already took off. The blankets are right here, folded in a stack, and there's no sign of her."

Will breathed a disappointed sigh. "Did she say anything about me?"

"What?" Jennifer asked, tiredly.

"Did Anne Rose tell you she met me?"

"Yes, Will. She told me a lot of things."

"Like what?"

"I don't know. She told me stuff I can't even remember. She told me she met you and some other old man name Mitchell. And then she went to Mike's restaurant."

"Mike's restaurant? You mean Carson's?"

"No, Mike's. She talked mostly about that. That dude Mike, the owner, brought her back into the kitchen and let her cook and everything."

Will let out a disappointed sigh. "And now she's not there?"

"No, she's not. She left a note and went home."

Will tried not to sound as deflated as he was. "Thank you for checking," he said to Jennifer. "I'm really sorry I woke you up."

"It's fine, Will. I'll talk to you later." She hung up, and Will sat there.

He and Anne Rose had exchanged phone numbers, and all he had to do was call her at her house. But he really hoped he would be able to catch her before she left town. He had gone to sleep thinking about her and he had dreamed about her.

57

But he had work to get done. It was Saturday, and he was technically off work, but he put a lot of effort into his job. He and his cousin, Evan, were in charge of expanded distribution at his uncle's hardware store. In the last year-and-a-half, the two of them had put ideas in play which had already increased the company's profit by fifty percent.

Will had reason to work hard as some of his pay was based on commission from sales. He was fully committed to making the business a success, and he was reaping financial gain because of it. But this morning he felt like driving straight to Houston. He hadn't said anything to Jennifer, but *who in the world was this Mike person?*

Will was so taken by Anne Rose during their time together that he couldn't understand how she could possibly have a more memorable encounter with the guy she met *after* him. It bugged him, but he went on with his day.

He finished up his work just after noon, and the first thing he did when he arrived home was call Anne Rose. There was no use in pretending that he would be able to wait and call her another day. It was hard enough to give her till noon to get back to Houston.

He dialed the number that Anne Rose had written on a napkin at the diner. She had taken time and care with writing it. She made her name nice and neat with perfect block print numbers below it. There were no questionable characters—no numbers that looked like other numbers. He called, hoping and praying that she would pick up.

"Hello?"

"Hey, Anne Rose?"

"Yeah."

"This is Will."

"Hey, Will. How are you? I was just thinking about you."

Will's heart ached when she said that. He felt like he might just fly through the air all the way to Houston—like his chest was literally pulling him in that direction.

"What were you thinking about?" he said.

"Well, lots of things, but I was wondering how it went last night. I wondered if y'all sang."

"What?"

"The birthday song. I wondered if you just got together to eat in celebration of the birthday, or if you actually sang the birthday song to them."

"What do you think we did?" he asked, smiling.

"Sing."

"Yes. My little cousin, Mac, even added the part about *and many more, on channel four, watch Scooby Doo, on channel two...*" Will sang the extra tag line of the birthday song, and Anne Rose laughed.

"I wonder who taught him that," she said. She was implying that Will had been the one to teach him since he sang it so well. She was actually right.

Will laughed at her for knowing that. "I might have taught him," he said... "Years ago, when he was like four."

"Well, now he's passing it on to the other four-year-olds."

"I wish you would have been able to be there," he said.

"Me too," she replied.

"You could have sang the birthday song with us."

They were quiet for a few seconds, but Will couldn't stop himself from saying what was on his mind.

"I called Jennifer this morning," he said. "I was going to try to catch you before you left, but she said you were... who's Mike? She said you were talking about a guy named Mike who cooked for you or something like that."

Anne Rose took a deep breath. It was so deep and audible that it seemed like it was in preparation to say something. Will waited to hear what she would say, but she just took another breath and made a moaning noise of hesitation. Finally, she spoke.

"I'm trying to think of a way to say it. Mike is a guy who I think might be a member of my family," she said. "There's new information that might be true about my family. It's family stuff and I'm just feeling it out. That's why I went to Galveston in the first place. Mike's an old man. He and his wife just wanted to meet me because they think we're related."

She took another deep breath. "They're nice people, but there have been lies told in the past, so there might be confusion if my parents knew I had gone there. If all this is true, then it means that one or both of my parents have been lying to me since I was born."

"Oof," he said.

"Yeah, I don't really want to think about that yet. I'm happy with my life the way it is, but I believed this Galveston story enough that I cared to check it out."

"I'm confused," he said.

"It's because I'm being confusing," she said. "I'm sorry. Basically, this guy Mike lives in Galveston, and I went there because I think he might be my grandpa, only I can't really tell anyone."

"Wow."

"Yeah, I've only met him and his wife. There's a son, and a daughter who has her own children, but I haven't met any of them. Just the grandma, and then last night I met her husband. I'm not talking to my parents about it. Not yet, at least. It's a conversation that would change things in my life."

"That's a big deal," Will said. "Are you not close enough to your parents to come out and ask them about it?"

"I don't know. Yeah, I'm close to them, but this is weird. They obviously didn't want me to know about it, or they would have told me by now. The grandma told me the first time we met that we could have a test done that would tell us for sure if we're related, but..."

"Are you going to do it?"

"I don't know. I'm tempted to. I like them. I feel like I might go down to Galveston to see them sometimes. The grandpa said he'd teach me how to cook."

"Come. That way you can see me again next time you come to town," Will said.

"Okay," she agreed.

"Okay? Is it that easy?" he asked. "All I had to do was ask?"

"I guess," she said. "I had fun with you yesterday."

He could hear her smiling, and he loved that sound. "Me too," he said.

"Next time, you can take me walking on the beach" she said.

"When?" he asked.

"Next weekend, maybe. Saturdays are good for me."

***

And that conversation was the beginning of a new relationship between Will and Anne Rose.

She started going to Galveston almost every weekend. They spent Saturday afternoons together, and they usually talked on the phone once or twice a week.

It was a friendship because that was all Anne Rose would allow it to be. Will was patient, and he never told Anne Rose how much he desired her. He acted nonchalant even though every time he saw her he wanted to take her into his arms and make her promise to never leave.

She was busy with finishing school and she had family issues to work through. All she needed was a friend, so that was what Will was to her. He found out that her family issues had to do with her biological father's real identity. His family lived in Galveston, but she was obviously more comfortable not sharing the specifics of who they were with Will. She told him more than she told anyone else, though.

Several times, her emotions surrounding that family stuff had come to a head, and she had been on the verge of telling her mother and father everything, but she always decided not to do it. Will was the only person who knew even this much of Anne Rose's secret, and he loved that she confided in him.

Chapter 7

Anne Rose

It was April now and I had gotten into a routine of traveling to Galveston almost every weekend. I told my parents I made some new friends there, and that was enough information to curb their curiosity.

Thanksgiving came and went, and then so did Christmas, New Year's, Valentine's Day, St. Patrick's, and Easter. Weeks and months passed, and I became close with the Elliots and with Will.

I drove there on Saturday mornings, and went home Saturday evenings—that way I didn't have to find a place to spend the night. Will and the Elliots had both offered at separate times to provide a place for me to sleep, but I didn't mind making day-trips.

I had a little routine. In the morning, I would go straight to the restaurant where Mike put me to work doing specific types of jobs and teaching me. Not all of it was glamourous. I did my share of scrubbing and cleaning, but Mike insisted on having quality food and an immaculate kitchen, and he wasn't willing to budge on that. I quickly learned to work smarter and not harder, and I started trying to limit my mess as I went along.

I would cook and learn and then eat lunch with Helen and Mike. We would eat whatever dish Mike and I prepared during our meeting. Helen always had picky things to say about it, and Mike would defend us, making an excuse or telling her she was wrong. They bickered, but I got used to it. I could tell they loved each other and me, and honestly, I loved them back.

It wasn't just about the cooking. I felt close to them because I knew in my heart that I was their granddaughter. I saw pieces of myself in them— physical attributes that were unmistakable.

So, my Saturday mornings were spent with the Elliots, followed by an afternoon with Will. They knew I had another friend in Galveston, but I was concentrating on other things when I was around them, and I rarely brought it up. I told Will some of the details of my relationship with the Elliott's, but I was never clear about their identity because I knew his family knew everyone in Galveston. I said their first names but not their last.

Will and I had gone out to eat a dozen times on Saturday evenings, but I never brought up their restaurant, and neither did Will, so we just didn't go there.

I liked it that way.

In the past few months, I had made relationships with the Elliots and with Will, and neither of the worlds ever intersected.

We were now well into spring. I would be graduating and getting a real job soon, so I knew my fairytale time in Galveston might have to end—or maybe not end completely, but change.

I couldn't go on avoiding the truth with my parents. In the last few months, I felt like something was putting added stress on them. My mom never mentioned it to me, but I didn't want to add to whatever it was. I constantly felt like I needed to either stop going down there to see the Elliots or come clean with my parents about it. It just never seemed like a good time. And I was scared.

But more than that, at this moment, I was desperate to get back to Galveston. It had been three weeks since my last trip. I missed once because my parents needed my help with something in the yard, and then the following week, I had a cold. So, I had missed two weeks in a row. I didn't realize how much I had grown to love all my Galveston people until I had to miss two trips.

During that time, I became frustrated and came really close to telling my mother everything. But I just couldn't bring myself to do it. I imagined the pain it could cause for my parents. I would be on the very edge of spilling my guts, and then I just couldn't get the words to come out of my mouth.

So, no one knew anything. And, again, I was headed to Galveston to live my double life.

I was currently happy with my situation, though. It was a beautiful spring morning and I was overjoyed to finally be headed south to see my Galveston people.

My easygoing mood lasted until about ten seconds after I walked into the restaurant.

"Your mother is coming," was the first thing Helen said to me when I walked in the door. She was looking straight at me, otherwise I would have assumed she was talking to someone else.

It felt like all the blood left my head at once. "Ma'am?" I said.

"Your mother. She called our home and said that she knew you were planning on coming here today. She said she'd leave right after you and get here moments after you arrive."

Helen looked serious. Mike was nowhere to be seen.

"Mike didn't talk to her," she explained. "I told him you and I were going to make lunch for him today. His birthday was last weekend."

"I know. I'm sorry I couldn't be here. I brought a present."

"Thank you," she said with a little smile. "I'm not sure if I did the right thing by not telling him what's going on. I just don't know how he'd do with meeting your mom. You know how he can be. I told him I wanted to come show you how to make my famous quiche."

There was a menu item called *Helen's Famous Quiche*, so I just nodded, knowing exactly what she was talking about.

"But are we really even making it? Are we still doing this? I mean, it seems like we're not going to be doing much cooking... with my mom coming. Is she really coming here?"

I was shaken. It felt surreal to say that.

"Yes, she is. And of course we're cooking. Your mom can just join us in the kitchen," she said resolutely.

Within ten minutes, my mother arrived. Prep chefs were already at work in the kitchen, and my mother followed us to the corner of the kitchen where Mike and I always worked.

It was unbelievably weird to go through the familiar motions with my mother and Helen there instead of Mike. For the first minute, Helen began getting her ingredients together while my mother and I stood there and watched her awkwardly. Finally, after what seemed like three hours but was a matter of seconds, my mother breathed a resigned sigh and spoke.

"So, uhh, Anne Rose, it was around Christmas, I think, when I realized why you were coming down here. It was close to that time. I saw you had a few extra gifts and then you came home with that necklace."

I blushed. Helen and Mike had given me a necklace, but I didn't even know my mother had noticed it. She hadn't acted like it.

Mom breathed another sigh. "I figured out why you were coming here and what you were doing, but I honestly thought it would be a phase. I told myself it was fine, that the Elliots had gotten in touch with you, and you would check it out, but then I saw that you didn't stop…" My mom trailed off randomly and stared at Helen. "I don't want to have to explain all this again. Where's Michael? Is he coming?"

"I've never met him," I said. My mom blinked at me like she was confused, and I stared at her. "Are you talking about Helen's husband or her son?" I asked. "They're both Michael."

"She's talking about my son," Helen said. "And he's not here. He lives in Houston. I never see him. I thought you knew that when you called this morning."

"No, it was just the only number that was listed. I assumed he was with you."

"No," Helen said. "It's just Mike Senior and I who've been getting to know the girl.

I stared at my mother, having no idea where to begin. "Is it true that Helen and Mike are my grandparents?" I gestured to Helen but stared at my mom.

"Yes," she said, gazing blankly at me and speaking slowly. "I had an affair with Michael that lasted a few months. I had lost a baby with your father, and I was depressed, and I… Michael was… I met Michael, and… uhhh… I'm sorry." She put her face in her hands for a second but then wiped at it like she was trying to get herself together.

"How do you know who my dad is if you were with both of them?"

"You can tell just by looking at you who your dad is," Helen said.

"I wasn't with your dad when I found out I was having you. We hadn't... we were fighting, and, I had only been with Michael."

"Does dad know?"

Mom nodded regretfully. "Not until a few months ago when I figured out where you were going. He had been the one to help me track you down, so I had to explain."

I imagined my dad hearing the truth.

I was suddenly overwhelmed.

I felt tears fill my eyes, and my mother took me into her arms.

"He doesn't care," she assured me. "I mean, he cared, and we had things to work out between us, but Anne Rose, please know that none of this is your fault. Your father is still your father. He still considers you his daughter, a hundred percent. It hasn't changed anything between you and him. He knows I'm here today and he wanted me to tell you that he loves you and nothing has changed, okay?"

I cried. I couldn't help it. Mom held me tightly, and I cried. I pressed the side of my face into her shoulder and covered it with my hand.

"Why didn't you tell us a long time ago?" I asked wiping my eyes.

"I'm so sorry," she said. "At first, I thought I had to hold the secret, and then, it just got too hard to decide when to... I just didn't. Anne Rose, I'm sorry.

I'm so sorry. I love you so much, baby girl, and I don't want you to feel like this makes you any less a part of our family."

"Yeah, but it makes her more a part of ours," Helen said in a matter of fact tone as she chopped an onion.

"I didn't want to believe that," Mom said to Helen. "But I think you might be right." She sighed. "I thought it was a phase, or that maybe Anne Rose felt obligated to come here. But these last weeks have proved me wrong. She stayed home, and I could tell she... (she looked at me) I could tell you missed it over here. I could see how excited you were to come here today, and I knew it was time for me to say something. Dad and I want you to know that we're here for you no matter what. You can come home and never see these people again, and we'll support you in that. Or you could continue getting to know them, and we'll support you in that too. When I came here today, I assumed Michael was part of all this."

"We haven't seen Michael in years," Helen said. "I talk to him now and again, but things aren't the same. He's been hurt and we've been hurt, and... he's never been a part of us getting to know Anne Rose. He's the one who told me about her, back last fall, but he doesn't know I called her."

My mom looked directly at me. "Well, baby, I just wanted to come here and check it out for myself.

I needed to make sure that everything was on your terms," she said.

"You could've just asked me about it at home instead of driving all this way," I said.

My mom started to say something and then she made an expression like she genuinely hadn't thought of that. "I guess I just wanted to come over here and see what the situation was."

I pointed at Helen. "I usually stand right there where Helen is standing. Mike teaches me how to cook."

Helen gestured to a nearby cupboard. "Anne Rose has an apron and a set of knives in there," Helen said. She looked at me. "You should get suited up and chop some ham for me."

"I'd love to see you work in the kitchen," Mom said. She reached up and wiped my wet cheek. "I'm so sorry, Anne Rose" she said. "I never did anything thinking it would hurt you. I always just wanted to protect you. It sounds crazy because I know I've made all sorts of mistakes in all this, but I wanted to do everything and say everything at the right time. I wanted to be honest with you, I just never knew how to do it, or when." My mom trailed off, her voice higher than usual as she fought back tears. "I'm sorry. I have no excuse other than to say that I was doing what I thought was best at the time. And here we are."

"Well, at least it came out before I croaked and didn't get to enjoy the girl," Helen said, causing my mom and me to laugh and cry at the same time.

After a few seconds of wiping my face and hugging my mom, I washed my hands and put on an apron. My mom put down her purse and came alongside us, watching the process.

It was a therapeutic start to my morning—secrets were exposed—forgiveness was requested and granted.

And we also prepared some tasty quiche.

Chapter 8

My mom and Helen got along so famously that we were able to tell Mike Elliot everything without there being a panic or uproar of any kind. Helen called and calmly told her husband the facts, and then we shared a beautiful brunch—three lovely ladies and Mike, all getting along great.

Mike had no choice but to go with the flow. We made it easy for him. We were making it easy for each other, too. All three of us were doing our best to bridge gaps with each other.

It was a wonderful morning. I knew things wouldn't be awkward with my dad when I got back to Houston, and that was a weight off of my shoulders. I also knew that both my mom and Helen were supportive of me continuing to come to Galveston to build relationships.

I loved my new adopted grandparents, and I loved learning how to cook. I was happy that everyone was fine with me continuing the routine.

We ate and talked, and healing took place.

I felt different when I left there.

I felt changed—like a weight had been lifted.

I felt like I could see and think clearer than ever.

I was truly happy and I couldn't wait to tell Will.

"I love you guys," I said moving to the edge of my seat at the thought of him. "I told my friend I'd be there at twelve-thirty." I could see that my mom was about to ask me a question, so I added, "We're going to the beach this afternoon."

"Okay, I need to be getting home anyway," Mom said.

And within five minutes, I was on the road, headed to Will's place.

I had never been so excited to see him. It had been far too long since we had been together.

My current mood brought on ooey-gooey, fairytale feelings that made me imagine greeting Will in a different way than I normally did. I got a little nervous when I thought about him.

Up until now, butterflies had not come into the equation with Will and me. I knew that if I went around letting myself get those, I would eventually lose Will since that was all he was interested in. I had chosen, back when we first met, to have Will as a friend and not a short-term boyfriend.

I reminded myself of that when I started daydreaming about him on my way to his apartment. I told myself to calm down, that I was just excited to see Will because it'd been so long. This was the truth. It had been far too long, and I was dying to see him. I had to keep myself from speeding to get there.

Will had an apartment near Bank Street where we had first met. Going to his apartment was something I had done lots of times during the past months. But today it felt different. I was nervous and excited to see him. I thought it might be on account of everything working out the way it did with my parents and the Elliots.

I hardly remembered ascending the stairs that led to his apartment.

I might have taken them two at a time.

I made it to the third floor and knocked on Will's door without even thinking about it. I should have given myself time to catch my breath before I knocked. I smiled at myself for being in such a hurry, and I tried to steady my breathing while I waited for Will to come to the door.

He opened the door seconds after I knocked, smiling the instant he saw me.

He looked amazing. He had on jeans and a fitted, broken-in t-shirt. It was white, and it made his skin look tan.

"Well, aren't you a sight for sore eyes?" he said.

"I was thinking the same thing about you," I replied.

I stepped forward as I was speaking, across the threshold and straight into his arms. I went there without hesitating, and he caught me, holding me firmly.

"Whoa," he said.

But he didn't let me go. We stood in his doorway and hugged tightly for several long seconds.

I felt tingling sensations all over my body. My skin was alive in all the places he was touching me, which was everywhere, since we were smashed against each other, hugging.

I pulled back when I realized how much I wanted him. I wanted him so much that I felt like kissing him right then. I almost did it. I laughed a little as I pulled back, adjusting my hair.

"I'm still out of breath because I ran up the steps," I said, saying anything.

Will was smiling as he walked backwards into his apartment, and I followed him inside after I closed the door.

Something was different. I didn't know what it was, but something was different, and I was in big trouble. Will smiled at me casually, noncommittally, like a friend would. But I no longer wanted him to do that. I wanted him to gaze at me longingly, like he wanted me.

But then I remembered that I was the one who had made him be casual and noncommittal. I was the one who taught him how to treat me like a friend. *Was there any way I could take back my request to be Will's friend and go for the short-lived version where he kisses me?* I had never wanted to kiss a man so badly as I wanted to kiss Will Castro right then.

He was looking at me and smiling, but I wanted him to focus on me in a different way. I was sorry I ever wanted to be his friend.

"I missed you," he said, going into his kitchen to finish what he was doing at the dishwasher.

"Oh, goodness, I forgot your quiche. I was so excited to get up here and see you that... just a second." I held up a finger. "I'll be right back."

Like light-footed lightning, I ran out of Will's apartment, down the stairs, out the door, and down the sidewalk until I found my car. I retrieved the box of food out of the passenger's side and bolted back down the sidewalk, into the building and up the stairs.

I gave the door a few light taps, but it was still cracked open from when I was there twenty-eight seconds before, and all I had to do was push it. I kicked off my shoes by the door and crossed to the kitchen, moving quickly.

"Whew, I had just caught my breath from coming in the first time," I said, smiling at myself as I rounded the corner of the bar and slid the box to him on the counter.

"What'd you make today?"

"Helen cooked today," I said. "We made quiche. It's sooo good. I'll put some on a plate for you."

"Thank you," he said.

"My mom was there," I said as I took a plate from the cupboard.

"Your *mom* was there?" he asked sounding shocked.

"Yes," I said. "She had known where I was going for a while, and finally, she just came over here with me."

"Oh my gosh, what happened?" he asked. He looked me over, trying to see if I was okay. "Tell me exactly. This is a big deal, Anne Rose. It's no wonder you're hyper."

I laughed and shook my head as I put a small portion of quiche on the plate and into the microwave. I was breathing more naturally now, and I went to stand right next to Will, feeling the need to be close to him.

"I am hyper. I'm heating up this quiche, and I didn't even ask you if you were hungry."

I turned his way. I was close to him, and I was staring straight into his eyes. It was as if a whole army of butterflies had been unleashed in my body at once. They were migrating, perhaps. It was at that moment that I realized why this feeling was referred to as butterflies in the first place. The fluttering sensation was physical. I had asked if he was hungry, and I stared at him during the seconds before he answered.

"Ye-yes, I'm hungry, Anne Rose," he said. He spoke hesitantly, staring at me with a cautious expression. His face. It was perfect. He saw me staring at him. I figured he knew something had changed in me. He could see right through me.

The microwave beeped, and I flinched but then quickly leaned the other way and reached out to grab his plate.

I took a fork from his drawer and set it on the plate next to the quiche.

Will took the plate and expertly cut a piece of quiche with the edge of the fork before taking a bite. "That's really good," he said, doing it a second time.

I watched him, wondering how in the world I had made it this long without seeing it. Goodness. *Was I really that preoccupied with my family that I couldn't see—I mean, even his chewing did it to me.*

I watched the muscles in his jaw flex as he ate, and I felt weak in the knees because of it. I had no idea what had happened to me. I came to the conclusion that absence must indeed make the heart grow fonder.

"This is sooooo good," he said, between bites. "Thank you."

"You're welcome," I said.

He took another bite. "Why are you staring at me like that?" he asked.

"Like what?"

"I don't know. You don't usually watch me eat."

"Yes, I do," I said. "I'm seeing how you like it. I always do that because I want to see how you like my food."

"I already told you I love it and you're still staring. Even right now, you're doing it."

His face shifted into an irresistible smile, and I compulsively leaned toward him, bumping into him. He was standing with his back toward the counter and I was facing the other direction. My movement caused our arms to touch briefly and he pulled back to stare at me.

"What are you doing?" he asked.

I was completely vulnerable to him. I felt vulnerability in the physical form of a warm, weak feeling in my core. I felt the urge to melt into his arms. If only he would grab me.

"Nothing. I'm just... checking you out."

"You're checking me out?" Will asked, pulling back and staring at me with a half-smile.

I thought about saying ten different things at that moment, but "Yes," was what came out of my mouth.

"Yes, you *are* checking me out?" he asked, cocking his head like he was clarifying.

"Yes," I said. "Is that okay?"

"Uhh... yeah." He looked me over, watching me watch him. "You look like you're..." He took another bite of quiche. "You're staring at me like you like me."

"I do like you," I said easily. "I wouldn't come see you every Saturday if I didn't like you."

"Yeah, but, other Saturdays you don't ever stare at me while I'm eating." He took another bite, and yeah, he was right, I was staring. His mouth, though. It begged to be stared at. He chewed, and I peeled my eyes off of his jaw and mouth and made eye contact with him before glancing away.

"I'm sorry," I said. "I think I was staring more than usual. I'm just... my mind's not on other things."

"Don't be sorry for that," he said casually. "I've been trying to get you to stare at me like that for months."

"You wanted me to?" I asked dazedly.

"Uhh, desperately," he said hoarsely.

"I guess I was carrying a load, worrying about all that parent-grandparent stuff, because everything just worked out, and then the first thing on my mind was... I was excited to tell you about it, and I haven't seen you in a long time, so I'm excited about seeing you. I'm happy. I feel happy, and I wanted to see you. I was happy when I thought about seeing you."

Will ate the last bite of quiche as I was talking, and just after that, he turned and set down the empty plate. "I'll be right back," he said surprising me.

He jogged toward the hallway, nimbly dodging some furniture on the way. Will had played every sport in school. I had seen him do athletic things, but never before had I felt so devastatingly attracted to him as I did today. It was the jeans and the way he moved in them.

I took a deep breath, and turned to rinse the plate he had just been using. There was nothing to rinse, he had eaten it all. But I ran the plate under water and put it and the fork into the dishwasher. I also put the box with the remainder of the quiche into the refrigerator.

I was closing the fridge when I heard Will's footsteps behind me. I turned and smiled at him.

"There's more of that quiche. I put it in the fridge for later."

"Thank you," he said. He sprang onto the counter, sitting up there and smiling at me like he was up to no good.

"What are you doing? Where did you go just now?" I asked, scanning his appearance.

"To brush my teeth," he said.

"To brush your tee—" I started to ask the question dramatically like I had no idea why in the world he would want to do that, but then it hit me. "Did you really?" I asked, grinning at him like I thought he must be joking.

"I did. Come here, I'll show you." Will licked his lip and then bit at it in a maneuver that had me dying to collapse onto him.

I was stunned, though, and couldn't make myself move. I didn't expect any of this to be happening just yet, right now.

I blinked.

Chapter 9

"Anne Rose," Will said.

"Yeah?" I asked. I was lost in thought. I had gotten to know Will during these months, and I knew him to be a talented, driven, smart, funny, loving man who was all about family. I loved all of those attributes. I had loved them all along. But now I felt like I actually loved the man who possessed them.

"You're stuck," Will said. He waved his hand in front of my face.

"I wondered why you would want to brush your teeth," I said.

He smiled casually, sitting on the kitchen counter, letting his feet dangle. His white teeth did look freshly brushed.

There was unmistakable mischief in his eyes, and I swallowed hard. The tension was thick between us. I could feel it. He was going to kiss me. My lungs seemed to function at half capacity. This was really happening, and I felt overwhelmed but also devastatingly excited.

"I thought you already knew why I brushed my teeth," Will said.

I blinked. "Because of the quiche?"

"Yeah, but that's not all," he said.

"I think I know, but you need to tell me so I can make sure."

"Well, it's kind of hard to tell you with you standing way over there."

"It is?" I asked shyly. I was only a couple of feet away, but I also thought it was too far.

"Yes," he said, sitting casually on the counter and staring at me.

I took two steps closer to Will, coming to stand right next to him. My side barely touched the edge of his leg. He was up higher than me since he was sitting on the counter. His legs were spread apart in a relaxed, easy posture, and in a maneuver that was really unlike me, I moved in front of him. I was technically situated between his legs, but he was positioned so far back on the counter that we were barely touching.

Will gazed at me, staring seriously at my new position. His mouth slowly turned upward in an easy smile. "What is going on here, Anne Rose?"

"I thought you were going to tell me what's going on," I said breathlessly. "You said it was hard to tell me from way over there, so I came over here."

His legs slowly came together, giving my sides a gentle squeeze. I smiled at him for doing that. "You're about to get yourself in trouble," he said, staring down at me. He leaned in, ducking and placing his face right next to mine. Our cheeks were gently touching. His mouth was near my ear. My heart pounded, and I put my hands on his knees to steady myself.

"I've been waiting for months," he whispered.

"You have?"

"Yes, Anne Rose. I have. You have no idea."

He spoke slowly and his voice was hoarse. I shut my eyes tight while a gut-clenching wave of urgency washed over me. I ached for him. I ached to be close to him. *Was he saying he had been feeling like this the whole time we had known each other?* I would feel really bad if that was the case because I was experiencing a physical pang.

Tentatively, I reached up, letting my fingertips touch the back of his neck. We weren't looking at each other. We were cheek to cheek. I let my fingers roam upward, running them slowly, deliberately through his hairline and into his hair. He leaned into my hand, which brought his head farther back, causing his cheek to rub against mine.

"You're going to give me a heart attack," he whispered.

I hadn't been expecting him to say that, and I let out a little laugh. He pulled back to look at me when I did that, and I made a short, whimpering, moan of disappointment. It was quiet and fleeting, and I didn't even know he heard me.

Will pulled back, sitting up and staring down at me with a curious stare. My hand, the one that had been on the back of his head was now resting on his shoulder. I was clearly holding on to him and I could tell he did not know what to make of it.

"Anne Rose, I should be a gentleman right now and make sure that you're not about to do anything you regret. You've had a big morning."

"You are being a gentleman."

"Am I? I don't know. I need you to tell me what you want." Before I could answer, Will swallowed and sat up straight, looking to the side and smiling a little. He took my hand and put it on his chest. "You are doing this to me," he said.

He assumed I could feel his heart beating because that was where he placed my hand. But I couldn't feel anything because my own blood was pumping about a million gallons a second.

"They said you would leave me once this happens," I said breathlessly. I didn't expect to tell him what Jennifer and Emily said, but it was a fear of mine, and it surfaced and came out of my mouth before I could stop it.

"What?" Will asked, looking offended.

"Oh, uhh, Jennifer and them were saying how, you know, maybe you didn't stay with a girl for too much longer after you kissed her or whatever. But I'm okay with it. I thought about it and I figure it's worth the gamble. So, I'm not saying I don't want it to happen or anything."

His expression had changed.

Why had I done this? We were so close to kissing. We were so close and I was definitely in the mood. Why had I gone and sabotaged it?

"I meant it as a good thing," I said.

"Oh, you mean you *want* this to be goodbye?" he asked.

"No, no, I just mean you should take it as a compliment. It means that I want it to happen enough that I'm willing to... I don't know what it means. I'm sorry. I shouldn't have said that. I'd like to go back to where we were a minute ago. Is there any way we could do that?"

Will looked me straight in the eyes. "One, don't compare yourself to anyone else. I've never been with anyone like you, so the outcomes will not be the same. You don't need to compare yourself. Two, Anne Rose, this kiss—this kiss that's about to happen—it's the first of a million."

He put his cheek near mine, and I took in an unsteady breath, feeling a bit like I might crack into pieces. "A million would take a long time," I whispered. I stared at the wall behind him, feeling overwhelmed.

"Well, when it's one at a time, you don't really notice how long it takes. You lose count."

"So far, it still needs to happen once," I said.

He let his cheek brush mine, and I rubbed him back, leaning into him in a soft, fluid motion.

"Have you wanted to do this before today?" I asked.

Will let out a laugh. His chest shook, and I felt his face flex in a smile as he pulled back just far enough to stare at me. "Yes, Anne Rose, I wanted this before today," he said, grinning and looking amused.

"I'm sorry," I said.

"Are you changing your mind?" he asked.

"No, no, I just feel bad that it took me so long."

Will moved. It was with torturous gentleness that he let his mouth touch mine. I whimpered. It wasn't intentional. I wasn't trying to be cute. I wanted this to happen so badly that I uncontrollably whimpered when it did.

The muscles in his legs tensed when I did that, and I felt them squeeze me gently while his mouth was still barely touching mine. We kissed softly. I counted five or six of them, but then I lost count when it kept happening again and again. We just stood in that kitchen and kissed—light gentle, perfect touches—the soft kind that told me he really cared about me.

We kissed what must have been a hundred times, but it felt like only once. I had no concept of time or space when I was kissing Will. The gentle touch of his mouth on mine was the definition of pure pleasure. They were all just gentle contacts on the mouth, and yet somehow, Will made the whole experience an adventure—like no two kisses were the same.

It was an intense few moments where I was standing still but I felt wave after wave of a new kind of thrill. I felt like I was bursting with love and excitement.

Maybe I was in love.

Maybe this was what being in love felt like.

After several long minutes of kissing gently, Will readjusted, taking me into his arms and hugging me against his chest. I hugged him back, feeling like I needed the moment to pull myself back to reality.

"Wow," I said absentmindedly.

"Yeah wow," he said. His voice was low and soft, and the sound of it caused me to hold him tighter. "I'm not complaining, but what gives, Anne Rose?"

I thought about how to answer his question. "I don't know. Is it too much? I'm sorry if it's too much all at once."

He held me tightly and took in a deep breath. I could feel his chest expand and fall as he breathed. Now that I was close to him, I never wanted to be anywhere else. *How did I ever get away with only seeing him once a week?* It didn't feel like that would be enough. I was already dreading saying goodbye to him.

"The last thing you need to do right now is apologize," he said.

I held onto him as I shifted, rubbing his chest with the side of my face, letting my nose touch his neck.

"You smell nice," I said.

"I knew you were coming, so I was trying to lure you in with my cologne."

I sniffed him. "It worked," I said.

"Tell me what happened with Helen and your mom," he said, holding me. I thought he might let go of me, but he didn't.

"My mom found out about it a while back. But she didn't say anything until she realized in the last couple of weeks that I really hated missing my trips to Galveston—that I wasn't going to give them up. She didn't even know my dad wasn't involved. She thought I was meeting him the whole time."

"It's crazy that she knew why you were coming here, though."

"I know. I didn't even know she was coming until I got to the restaurant and Helen told me about it."

"And it went good? No fighting?"

"No. It went great. Mom said she came to tell me she supported me and that she was sorry if she had handled it wrong all these years. She saw how much I hated missing my trips lately, and she followed me over here this morning to tell me all that. Helen knew about it before I did. My mom had talked to her at home, and she ended up meeting me at the restaurant. Then Mike came, and it was all really cordial and adult-like. Everyone wanted me to be okay."

"Good," Will said. "They should want that. You guys should have done that a long time ago."

I shrugged. "Now I wish we would've. But I just didn't know how everyone would react. It makes sense now, though. I remember some arguing with my parents around Christmas. I had no idea all that was going on."

Will pulled back far enough to look down at me. "What happened at Christmas?" he asked.

"That's when they found out where I was going and my mom got exposed."

"Oh, you mean your dad didn't know about any of this before that?" Will asked.

"No."

"Whoa."

"No kidding," I said. "My mom apologized for that, too. She apologized a lot and cried several times, but I was ready to accept the information and move forward. Helen was too, obviously."

"What if you did all this and it wasn't even true?" he asked after taking a second to let things sink in.

"Oh, it is," I said. "They had proof."

"Who did?"

"Helen and Mike."

"What proof?" he asked.

"A DNA test. She took some of my hair during our very first meeting at Denny's and had a test done."

"Behind your back? That's kind of weird. Is that even legal?"

"I don't know, but she didn't look at it," I said.

"What?"

"She sent it off and got it back, but she never looked at the results. She said that by the time they came back, she and Mike had already decided they loved me and that I was their granddaughter, so there was no reason to look at it."

"So, they haven't seen it?"

"Well, now they have," I said. "She called Mike and told him to bring it when he came, and we opened it right there in the restaurant."

"And it's true?" he asked.

I nodded. "We opened it together and looked at the results."

"Wow, you really had a big morning."

I laughed. "Yeah," I said. "And a big afternoon," I added.

Will knew I was talking about him, and he smiled and bent down to bury his face in my neck. "That tickles," I said, trying not to squirm. He pulled back and leaned to the side.

"Do I finally get to meet these people, now that you're not worried about your mom finding out?"

"Yes, of course," I said. "Do you want to meet them?"

"Yes. And I want to eat some more of that food you bring over here. You should take me to their restaurant sometime."

"I will. You'll love it. You've probably eaten there. It's a big place. A lot of people go there."

"What's it called?"

"Elliot's."

"Elliot's *on the seawall*?"

"Yes."

Will stared at me.

"What?" I asked.
"You're joking."
"No, I'm not."

Chapter 10

I leaned back, pulling away from Will a little bit. It sounded like he couldn't believe the name of the restaurant when I said it. He even asked me if I was joking and I had to reassure him I wasn't.

"Why would I be joking?"

"I, uh, I, when you said you were cooking... I always pictured it as some tiny little hole-in-the-wall place."

"That's because we were always in this one little corner of the kitchen so we wouldn't get in the way of the lunch prep. What's wrong?"

"Nothing. I just... nothing. I didn't know it was that place. My family... so, your real dad is the son of those people? The Elliot's? I know that restaurant. I think we know those people."

"Yes. Michael Elliot. I thought maybe I should keep everything a secret since their relationship with Michael is strained. They have a daughter with a family, and I just thought we were keeping things under wraps, but today Helen and Mike insisted they didn't mind if people know who I am. We talked about it today, and Helen said I should take my friends over there to eat anytime we want. She said we get the family discount." I smiled at him and raised my eyebrows. "Plus, I'm learning how to cook," I said. "I don't have any grand notions that I'll take over the restaurant or anything, but I don't care about that. It's just cool that they love me and want to get to know me."

"Yeah," Will agreed. "That's awesome. I'd love to meet them sometime." He opened his mouth to say something, but then he stopped himself, making a little noise as he hesitated.

"What?" I asked seeing that he almost said something. I wanted him to be happy and comfortable, but he looked a little concerned.

"I'm... it doesn't matter at all to me. I couldn't care less... but I think those people don't like my family very much."

"Huh?" I asked, weakly. I had heard Helen badmouth a certain family... but surely it couldn't be the... "She said it's the Grahams," I said.

He nodded. "My family is the Grahams."

Even as he said it, the truth hit me. I don't know how I hadn't realized it before. Will's cousins, who I had known as "the twins" Jenny and Josh, were Grahams. That was their last name. I had met different members of his family at different times in the last few months. I had met the twins before, but I hardly remembered their last name and I definitely didn't make the connection.

"I always think of your family as the Castro's and the Kings," I said.

"Yeah, Aunt Laney used to be a King. She's Uncle Daniel's sister. She used to date Michael Elliot before she married Uncle James, and she had a big fight with... well, you might even know. I think that's why he, Michael, doesn't live here."

"Yeah, I know," I said, feeling sick to my stomach.

"Look, Anne Rose, that means nothing to us. I don't care about old grudges. As far as I'm concerned, it doesn't matter."

"Really?" I asked. "I can't believe the *one family* she talked about happens to be yours. I never would have thought that. I honestly pictured the Grahams as some back-woods, vile-old ruffians. She made it seem like they destroyed my dad and ruined the whole family. I thought they were just running amuck in this city. I kept thinking I'd come across some crazy-old-Grahams at the beach one day."

Will laughed. "I thought the owner of Elliot's were lunatics." He shook his head, staring at me with a gentle smile. "But that's old stuff," he assured me. "That doesn't mean you and I can't be—"

"Of course we can be together," I said, cutting him off before I was even sure about what he was going to say.

Will smiled at my response, and I felt incredibly thankful that he didn't care who my grandparents were. I hadn't realized how much I wanted Helen, Mike, and the restaurant in my life until a few seconds ago when I thought I'd be faced with the decision of choosing them or Will. There was no question that I would have chosen Will, but I would have been sad about being put up to it.

The way Helen talked, it was a Hatfield-McCoy situation with the Elliots and the Grahams. I had no idea Helen was talking about the same Laney Graham I had met with Will last Christmas and again a few weeks ago. That was insane. I learned her name and never even came close to making the connection.

"I've mentioned the restaurant by name to a couple of people in your family," I said. "I mentioned it one time to Tara, and another time to your Dad. They both told me not to eat there. I thought they just didn't like it. I couldn't understand. I thought maybe one of y'all got food poisoning or something."

"Yeah, no, we don't eat at Elliot's," Will said. "That's not even... I've never even been there in my life."

"Well, yeah, you have—take out, at least. Every Saturday."

"That's insane," he said. "I pictured y'all cooking in a tiny little kitchen, like this." He looked around indicating the kitchen we were standing in. "I actually pictured it in a little house—like a tiny café. Elliot's, huh? I've been missing some good food all these years."

"Do you think it's really no big deal? Is it just that simple? Do we just act like we don't know that our families hate each other?"

Will let out a little laugh. "Well, I'm definitely not giving you up over some old grudge," he said. "That stuff has nothing to do with us."

"Maybe it has a little to do with me." I bit the inside of my lip, feeling shy. "Since your aunt Laney might feel different about me now, if she knew my dad was… " I trailed off but then continued, "Do you think it's okay?"

Moments ago, I thought I had just resolved all the drama and tension in my life, and now I was sad that these new, unwanted, unfavorable connections were being made. Will adjusted me in his arms.

"It'll have to be okay," he said. "I don't think I'd be able to give you back after I just got you."

He propped himself on the counter and looked down at me, squeezing my sides with his knees again. I reached out and held onto him. I just grabbed him around his waist and hugged him. He was solid. I had held onto him before, a few times when he was showing me some boxing, but I had never noticed the feel of his body like I did today. I was so happy that he didn't want to give up. I didn't want to give up, either.

Doubt entered my mind when I thought of how Jennifer and the other ballerinas described Will as a player, but I was able to talk myself out of worrying when I remembered Will telling me that I shouldn't compare myself to other women. He looked me in the eyes and told me that I was different, and I had believed him when he said it. For the rest of the day,

I had to recall that conversation and reassure myself every time doubt would creep in.

Thankfully, Will did a good job of convincing me how he felt about me. We spent all day together and the whole time, he never lost contact with me. He wasn't overly gushy or annoyingly doting, but things had changed with us. Will looked at me differently, and he constantly held my hand or held onto me in some way. He saw that I looked at him in a new way, and he went with it.

We went to the beach first, and then we went by his cousin, Evan's. Usually, I left Galveston by around 6pm on Saturdays, but it was currently 7:30pm and we were just leaving Evan's house. He and his wife, Izzy, had recently bought a house. I had been to their old place, but never to their new one.

We cooked and ate dinner with them.

Izzy liked to cook, but she was open with her kitchen and loved advice, so I got in there with her and showed her a few things I had learned from Mike. It was fun talking to her, and I learned new things just by getting in there with her and answering her questions.

I had talked to Izzy a few other times, but never quite as much as I did tonight. Will and I spent three hours over at their house. Aside from the time I was with Izzy in the kitchen, Will and I were inseparable. We smiled at each other, and stared at each other, and stood close to each other all afternoon.

We had built a relationship during the last few months. We had a rapport. We had inside jokes, and we knew about each other's likes and dislikes. We had that foundation built already, so adding a layer of attraction felt easy—it felt natural. I cared for Will as a person. I loved his outgoing personality and his sweet, tenacious spirit.

I stared at him while he drove home from Evan's. We were talking so I didn't feel weird about looking at him. I reached for his hand and it felt like the most perfect hand that had ever been created. It was big and slightly work-hardened. I held it on the way back to his apartment. My car was parked there, and I would undoubtedly be leaving soon.

I felt pain in my chest at the thought.

"I'll see you next week," I said.

"Are you leaving right this second?" he asked.

"No, I was just assuring myself that I'd be seeing you in a week, so I said it out loud. It seems too long."

"Come back tomorrow," Will said instantly. "Stay the night. Stay with Jennifer, or at my sister's or my parents'. Stay the night and come eat lunch with my family. It's Sunday. My dad's barbequing."

"I've been wanting to try some of your dad's barbeque, but I can't. I have the girls in the morning, and I had to miss last week because I had a cold. I promised them I'd be there."

Will groaned and pulled my hand into his lap, pulling my arm, causing me to lean over the console, which I did readily. Will knew that I volunteered with fifth grade girls at my church, so he didn't ask me to explain what I was talking about.

"I wish I could," I said. "I really do, Will. I've never been so torn."

"Don't worry about it," he said. "Go be there for your girls. I actually love that you feel committed to that. I forgot about it when I asked you to stay."

"I love that you asked me to stay," I said. "Thank you for inviting me."

Will still had a hold of my hand, and he placed it on his own chest where he left it while he let go to make a turn.

"You're always welcome here," he said. "It doesn't matter what day. It doesn't have to be the weekend."

"Same with you in Houston," I said. "You're always welcome to come see me tomorrow." I smiled. "My dad won't be barbequing, but my grandma picks up fried chicken. It's no big deal. It's not a big family thing like you guys have, but you're more than—"

"I'd love to," he said.

"You *would?*"

Will smiled at my surprise.

"You're coming to Houston?"

He could see how excited I was and he nodded wearing an amused grin. "Yes, I'm coming to Houston."

Chapter 11

Will

Two days later

Will stopped by his parents' house for breakfast the following Monday morning. He had spent an incredible weekend with Anne Rose, and he was on cloud nine because of it.

He was in love.

He had hopelessly devoted thoughts about her. Just her name, for instance—Anne Rose. He never thought he would love a woman with that name. It was a rare, beautiful name, just like the woman herself. And her eyes, her yellow-green eyes.

She was extremely dangerous to him. Will was destroyed. He would give up anything for her. He was in love to a degree that he didn't even know was possible. He was in love to the point where he whistled absentmindedly. He was literally whistling when he walked into his parents' house.

"You're chipper this morning," his dad said. Billy Castro had not-so-long-ago been a world champion boxer, but he was the one with the apron on when Will came in.

Will's mother, Tess, was sitting at the bar in her pajamas with a cup of coffee. He went to his mom first.

"I am," Will said to his dad.

"He went over to Houston yesterday," Tess explained. "He was with his little friend over there."

"She is not, definitely not my friend. Not anymore," Will said, straight-faced.

"Why? Did y'all have an argument?"

"No, no, I'm saying she's not my *friend*." Will went into the kitchen to greet his dad, wash his hands, and get his plate as he spoke. "She is way more than my friend. I love her, y'all... I seriously... I'm in love."

"I knew that was coming with this girl," Billy said.

"I did too," Tess said. "I told your dad that right away, but then it seemed to, you know, with her being in Houston, I just assumed you were just friends."

"We were," he said. "We had never even held hands or anything that whole time, all those months, and then Saturday she came over and... hang on, let me pray..." Will closed his eyes for a second, pausing in silent prayer before opening his eyes and taking a bite of the food his father had handed him. "Anyway, so, she had been dealing with some family stuff, and once that got sorted out, it was like she came over, and things were different between us. I always loved her, but now that she doesn't have the weight of that family stuff happening anymore, she's just... I just have to have her."

Tess made a squeal of approval which morphed into her humming the tune of, *so this is love,* from Cinderella. Will didn't get her reference, he just saw that his mother was happy with the news.

She really liked Anne Rose. Billy did too. He had several long talks with her. They both loved to cook, which connected them off the bat. As a professional athlete, Billy had always paid attention to his nutrition, and they also had that in common. Will was happy to see his parents smiling about it.

Tess was overjoyed to see her baby boy whistling over a sweet young lady. She thought he looked handsome and she loved seeing him with a spring in his step. Tess was inspired. Seeing Will like that inspired her to make a painting of young love.

"So this is love, hmm, hmm, hmm, hmmm, so this is love...." She sang softly as she got off of her barstool. Will, having never paid attention to Cinderella, still didn't get it.

"Thanks, Dad," Will said, around a mouth full of breakfast hash. "It's really good. I like the avocados on there."

"You should taste this juice," his mom said crossing into the kitchen as if she was going to get some for him. "It's carrots and apples and a little ginger. We made it last night with the juicer."

"Sounds good," Will said.

"It is good," Billy agreed.

"Anne Rose likes ginger. She used it on something a while back that I liked... maybe fish, I can't remember. It makes sense that it would be fish since it came from a seafood restaurant."

Will knew in his heart that he was about to drop a bomb with his parents, but he hoped to slip it by them in conversation. He was setting himself up for that.

"She's always at her grandparents' restaurant, cooking with them... it's that seafood place on the seawall, Elliot's."

Will tried to say it quickly, calmly, and nonchalantly. In his mind, he would just say the name of the place like it was nothing, and they would all blow past it and start talking about something else.

But what actually happened was completely different. What actually happened was way more dramatic than that. Tess dropped the glass of carrot juice and it shattered all over the floor. Her muscle twitched, and the glass slipped out of her hand when she heard her son say the name of the restaurant.

There were a few seconds of chaos where Tess yelped in surprise, and then the shattering of the glass took place. Afterward, Tess looked around guiltily. It wasn't a hundred percent carrot juice, but there were enough carrots in there to give the white tile floor a thick orange coating.

Will could see the mess, and he instantly set down his food to go help.

"Don't worry about it," Billy said putting a hand in the air to tell Will to stop. "I'll get it. I have a broom and dustpan right in here. Don't move, babe, I see glass next to your feet." Tess stayed still, and Will sat back down, seeing his father spring into action.

"So, is Anne Rose a cousin to the Elliots?" Billy asked, in a casual tone that was meant to assure his wife it wasn't that big of a deal.

"She's their granddaughter," Will said. "Michael's daughter."

Tess's feet stayed still, but she started wiggling uncontrollably, tiny little motions from side to side. "No, no, no, no, no," she said, lightly, shaking her head. Her face was serious. "No, baby, Will, no."

"What do you mean, *no*?"

"I know you think that might work, but that would never, ever... I didn't even know Michael *had* a daughter." she paused and stared straight at Will, looking straight into his eyes, staring like she was lost in thought.

"Mom, what do you mean that would never work?"

"That would never work," she said plainly.

"Well, it is working. It does work. I just told you I was in love with her. We have a bond. She and I both—"

"No, no," she said, cutting him off. Tess was normally easygoing, but she was obviously distraught. "Since it's right here at the beginning of all this, you can go ahead and cut it off and just, you know, you can find somebody else."

"Babe," Billy said.

"What?" Tess asked, glancing down at her husband as he swept. Will could see that his mother was truly flustered by this information. She stared at Billy with a straight face.

"That's mean," Billy said. "He just came in here telling us that he's in love."

"Yeah, but it's day one," she said. "I think that's a good thing. He can go ahead and stop it before—"

"It's not day one," Will said. "I've been with her since November."

"Not like this," his mom said. Her expression softened and she gave him a regretful smile. "It might not seem like it, but it's a blessing that we found this out so early."

"You're talking like it changes things."

"It does change things," Tess said. "It should. You can't be with Michael Elliot's daughter."

"Babe," Billy warned.

"Yes, I can," Will said. "I'm sorry mom, I don't mean to talk back or disagree with you or whatever, but I don't even know anybody named Michael Elliott. That old stuff with him and Aunt Laney doesn't mean anything to me."

"Don't let Aunt Laney hear you say that," Billy said. "Or Aunt Abby for that matter. There was a lot going on with that man and Aunt Laney. Mrs. Elliot made life hard for Laney."

"Yeah, well, Mrs. Elliot thinks Aunt Laney was the one who made life hard."

"Will, you know your Aunt Laney. Do you actually think she would…"

"No, I'm just saying, there's two sides to things. Plus, Anne Rose doesn't even know Michael. Apparently, the grandparents don't talk to their son much. You don't know what they've been through."

"He's right," Billy said. "We don't know the whole story."

He swept the last bit of debris from around Tess. She moved when he finished avoiding the juice and, thanking him for taking care of the glass.

"Be careful," Billy said. "Where are you going?"

"To get the mop and bucket." Tess peeked into the broom closet before crossing to the sink with the bucket in her arms. She filled the bucket with water, thinking of what she wanted to say to her son next.

"Okay," she said calmly. "I'm sorry about the mess and I'm sorry if anything I was saying sounded mean or hurtful. I don't mean to over react or come across that way. It's just that I've spent a few days on this earth, Will, and sometimes in life things feel more permanent than they are. I can understand that you like this girl, but you have to consider family Christmases, weddings, your *own* wedding. You know? You have to step back and consider the whole package. I wouldn't normally say much about your choice in women. I know you're stubborn like me and that me saying something will only make you want to do it, but I really feel like I should step in on this one. I honestly wouldn't judge a girl for much. You can bring anyone here. I don't care about their size, or the color of their skin or hair, or her money. I would only step in if I felt like you were choosing somebody who was against the Lord."

"She's not though. She loves the Lord."

"Well, good. That part's good, I guess. But she's still Michael Elliott's daughter. That and hating the Lord are pretty much the only two reasons I would advise you against her."

"Mom, please, don't even compare those two things."

"No, Will, I'm serious. That would be really hard for both of you." Tess shook her head. "I don't think Helen Elliot would claim her if she knew she was dating... does she know you two are dating? Does Ms. Helen know about y'all?"

"I don't know, maybe, probably," Will said.

"And she's *okay* with it?" Tess asked, looking completely shocked.

Will hated that it was such a big deal to his mom. He didn't expect her to know the lady's first name. And, honestly, he expected his dad to step in more than he was.

Will crossed the kitchen with his plate. "Thank you," he said. "Sorry about the spill. And I'm sorry if it's seems stressful right now, but I'm warning you, I'm not planning on giving up Anne Rose. I want the rest of my life to be like the last two days."

Tess sighed thoughtfully as she finished moping.

"I think she's a really sweet girl," Billy said. "And beautiful."

A few seconds later, Tess let out a long sigh/moan type sound like she was just realizing something. "Oh, my gosh, her eyes," she said.

"I knowww," Will agreed. "They're amazing."

"I can't believe I sat there and talked to her about her green eyes and I didn't think of Michael Elliot. I even knew she's been going to cook somewhere. I just never dreamed it would be Elliot's."

"Me neither," Will said. "I told her we never, ever eat there."

"It's more than just not eating there, Will. Way more than that. Does she know Helen hates us?"

"A little," Will said with a shrug. "But it's not that big of a deal. I just don't think it's a big deal at all."

Tess shook her head. "I bet you ten dollars Helen Elliot does not know she's seeing you."

"Mom, honestly, after yesterday... and the day before, I realize that it won't matter what Mrs. Elliot or anyone else thinks. I honestly don't care who Anne Rose's dad is. To me, she's my girl. I'm not worried about whose daughter she is or whose granddaughter. I'm worried about who *she* is. And I know I want to be with her. So, the quicker everybody gets over it, the better."

Chapter 12

Anne Rose

A month later

My life had changed drastically during the last six months. And, the thing was, I had more significant changes still to come. I had just graduated, and now I was faced with deciding what to do next. Now that the time was here, I was pretty sure I would be moving to Galveston.

I would work at the restaurant, which turned out to be a dream job for me. I had so many things I wanted to do there. In the last month, since things came to the surface with my mom, I had been free to really think about what I wanted to do for a job, and honestly, the idea of cooking food at Elliot's and eventually running it seemed like a dream career for me. Plus, the love of my life was in Galveston, so it was a no-brainer that I would move there in that regard.

Will Castro was, in every way, the man of my dreams. I watched him in his work life and his family life, and it inspired me. I wanted to build a family with him. In the last month, I had gone to Galveston every Saturday, just like I had done all along. Will came to Houston once a week (usually on Wednesdays) to see me, too, but Saturdays had remained the same.

I had spent time with the Elliots in the morning and with Will in the afternoon, but they hadn't met each other yet. Will wasn't worried about Helen's reaction to him, but he suggested that we wait to make the introduction after my finals and graduation so that I could relax and not stress about it.

Helen and Mike knew I had a boyfriend, and I told them specific things about Will, but I intentionally left out certain names that would tip them off to who his family was. I wasn't scared to tell them, but wanted to make the introduction in person so they had to look into Will's eyes and see for themselves how wonderful he was.

In the past month, I had opened my heart to the Elliots in a way I wasn't able to do before they met my mother. I developed a loving relationship with them. I was seriously considering moving in with them after graduation. Helen and Mike had a guesthouse, and they insisted they would love to have me stay in it.

And suddenly, I was finished with school, and it was time for me to decide. With finals and graduation happening, I had a hectic month. And now it was over, and I was headed to Galveston with basically a one-way ticket. Really, I was just going for the night, but I had wrapped up all of my responsibilities in Houston, so my mindset had changed. My job at the bookstore ended with the semester, so I had no school or job holding me in Houston anymore. At the moment, me living in Galveston seemed like the right plan. I would still be close to my mom and dad, and I'd be able to see them anytime.

The only reason I hadn't already told Helen and Mike that I had decided to move there was because I hadn't introduced Will to them yet. I guess somewhere in the back of my mind, I was leaving myself an out in case they didn't accept him.

But, I wasn't worried about it. I was convinced that they would love him once they met him and it would all work out.

Tonight, we would see.

I was a little nervous but mostly excited.

I glanced at the clock on my dashboard as I pulled into the parking lot at the restaurant. I was celebrating my graduation, so I had come in on Friday at five o'clock for a small dinner celebration with the Elliots starting at six. I was meeting Helen and Mike at the restaurant at five and we had plans to visit for an hour before their daughter, Megan, and her family arrived to eat with us. I told Will to meet us there between five-thirty and six as well.

I had met Megan (my aunt) twice before. She knew I was Michael's daughter, but when we met, she didn't say anything to me about it. We talked about me loving to cook and the fact that I was thinking of moving to Galveston to work at the restaurant, but neither of us mentioned Michael. I could see her staring at my face, though—my eyes—and I could tell what she was thinking. I was happy to see Megan tonight and especially excited that they would all get to meet Will.

I had plans to spend the night in Helen and Mike's guesthouse and then have a normal Saturday where I made food with the Elliots in the morning and spend the afternoon and evening with Will before heading back to Houston.

I was in a good mood and feeling like the possibilities were endless as I walked into the back door of the restaurant. I smelled garlic and fish and rice and spices, mixed with the smell of wood and salt air.

"There she is!" Helen said to me when I walked into the office. I had parked in the back and come in through the kitchen door since I knew they'd be waiting for me in the office. Helen had made it her own little living room in there with a couch and television.

"What are y'all doing?" I said, coming in and smiling at both of them.

"The five o'clock news just came on," Mike said.

"Well, turn that off. That's not as exciting as our surprises!" Helen said, leaning over to take the remote from Mike. She muted the television, and he gave her a disappointed glare but it quickly changed to a smile when he looked at me. I went to him for a hug.

"Hey, Anne Rose, congratulations on graduation yesterday. Helen and I wished we could be there."

"Oh, I know, it's okay. I just walked up there when they called my name. It took all of twenty seconds."

"And at least we get to give her the surprise," Helen said. "And Anthony got some fresh snapper at the market today."

"Oh, man, I can't wait," I said. I meant it. I loved snapper, and they knew it. "Is that my surprise?" I asked feeling happy.

"Heavens no!" Helen said. "It's way bigger than that."

"What?" I asked. looking at her with a confused expression.

"There's two of them... three... come on. I'll show you number one first, and then we can go outside and see number two."

She took me by the arm, pulling me along with her as she walked out of the office. I glanced behind us to make sure Mike was coming, which he was. He fumbled to find his glasses and catch up with us, closing the office door behind him.

"Where are we going?" I asked.

"To the bar," Helen said.

I glanced all around as we walked out there, trying to find something that looked like a surprise... but it just looked like a normal Friday. There were some customers, but none of them looked familiar. It definitely wasn't a surprise party, thank goodness.

We walked all the way over to the end of the bar. I recognized the guy standing behind it, but he was further down, talking to a customer. He turned our way, noticing the owners and looking like he was doing his best to get to us.

Helen waved him off. She reached out, taking a menu from the stand. She placed it in front of me with a smile.

"Are we eating already? I told my boyfriend to be here at—"

"No, no, we're waiting for Megan. I told her six o'clock. No, open it." She shoved the menu in front of me, and I opened it, expecting to find a graduation card inside.

It was just a menu. Nothing else was in there. There was one page in the center, and I flipped it to see if there was a card stuffed into the other side. Nothing.

"It's on the first page," Helen said.

"About three-quarters of the way down," Mike added.

My gaze shot to that section.

"And it's just the beginning," Helen said from over my shoulder. "With your talent, the whole menu might be yours eventually."

I could hardly hear her because halfway through her sentence, my eyes fell on to a new menu item.

Anne Rose's Fish Tacos: $11.00

Delicious but guiltless - grilled snapper tacos with Anne Rose's own slaw and special sauce. (You'll want to take some of this sauce home with you.)

Tears filled my eyes as I read it. "I thought you said that sauce was just *okay*," I said, looking straight at Mike, blinking back tears.

"Okay enough to sit in that kitchen for two days and figure out how you made it," Helen said.

I laughed at that. "I had all the ingredients out when I was working on it."

"I know," Mike said. "I saw them. I kind of saw your process, too. But it took me two days to get the proportions right and get consistent with the process."

I playfully pushed at Mike's shoulder with my own. "Why didn't you just ask me, I would have told you exactly what I did."

"I wanted to figure it out," he said. "And I wanted to do this," he gestured to the menu. "I'm honored to have that dish on my menu," he said. "I'm not just putting it on there because you're my granddaughter. It's a good dish. We've already had several people order sauce to go. I told Helen we need to bottle it."

"What about the tacos?" I asked.

"Oh, yeah, we've been selling them since Wednesday," Mike said.

"What's that?" Randy, the bartender, asked when he walked up and caught Mike's comment.

"She was asking if we'd sold any of those fish tacos," Helen said.

"Oh, boy, have we! I sold some just now, as a matter of fact. I need to go put in that order. Can I get you three anything?"

"No, we'll be sitting in the dining room later," Helen said. "We were just coming to show Anne Rose her first menu item."

"Oh, yeah, is that yours?" Randy asked.

"Yes, sir," I said, smiling.

"Well, congratulations. And good job." Randy said. "I ate some yesterday. They're really tasty. It's my new favorite."

"Oh, wow, thank you," I said. I could not stop a huge grin from spreading across my face. I clutched the menu to my chest hugging it. "I love it so much!" I said, looking back and forth from one to the other. "Thank you," I said again. "This is seriously the best gift ever. I feel like I need to take one of these home and frame it."

"Thank you for making good food," Mike said.

"And for being a good girl," Helen agreed. "I can't believe you made the honor society. Did they give you an extra sash to wear?"

"Yes ma'am, they did. I don't have the pictures developed yet, but I'll give you one once I pick them up."

"Well, I should hope so," Helen said, teasing me. Her expression grew even more excited. She wore wide eyes and a huge smile. "And now for the *second surprise*. What time is it?" She looked at Mike. "Is it the right time?"

"It doesn't matter what time, hon, I told you that. We just go out there when we're good-n-ready."

"Well, I hope it's all situated," she said, staring at her husband.

"It is. I told you. Just go out the front door."

"Oh, now I'm really wondering what you guys are up to," I said as we walked toward the front of the restaurant. "Is it fireworks?" I asked, racking my brain.

"Fireworks?" Helen asked, her voice sounding sharp with playful surprise. "Fireworks!" she continued, laughing. "Where would you get that?" She was in the best mood.

"You. You were asking if it was time, and when I think of it being *time* for something that has to be outside, I think of fireworks."

"No," Mike said. "It's not fireworks. It's not even dark."

"Oh yeah," I said absentmindedly as we continued walking towards the door. I had never seen Helen walk so quickly. She basically scurried to the door. I was so curious that I was right there with her, and we made it to the door quickly.

"Come on," she said, motioning to Mike who wasn't moving quite as fast as we were. We stepped outside, and walked off of the wooden deck and onto the sidewalk. Sarah, one of the hostesses, was standing in an open parking spot right in front. She walked our way, and I realized she was staring straight at me.

"Congratulations," she said.

"Oh, thank you," I said.

"I'm jealous," she added, smiling and waving at me and she walked past me toward the restaurant.

I wondered if she was jealous of me graduating college or getting my name in the menu. I didn't realize for another few seconds that she was talking about something else completely.

Helen was bouncing up and down like a kid at Christmas. Mike grinned and nudged me with his elbow, and when I looked at him, he pointed down the street.

I glanced in the direction he was indicating, and I saw a brand-new, gorgeous BMW convertible headed our way.

Chapter 13

"What's going on?" I said, stepping back and looking at both of them with a serious and confused expression.

Helen's face contorted and she began crying. Mike stood beside her, holding her around the shoulders, looking like he was struggling to hold back tears as well. He pointed to the car that was being pulled into the parking spot right in front of me. There was a man driving it. He was someone I didn't recognize. He had on a BMW hat and a pair of sunglasses, and I immediately assumed that he was a car salesman and that the car was *mine*.

"What's going on?" I repeated, not wanting to make those assumptions out loud.

"It's yours," Mike said, gesturing to the car, which was now parked right in front of me.

"G-go over there!" Helen said, crying. "Go see it, go see it!"

She was more moved at this moment than I had ever seen her before. Under other circumstances, I probably would have insisted that this was too great a gift and they couldn't possibly buy it for me. But Helen was so excited that I couldn't get past her reaction enough to think straight.

"Go, go s-see it. Get the keys from the man," she said, crying and talking high-pitched and wiping at her face with one hand as she urged me forward with the other.

She pushed my shoulder, causing me to step down off the sidewalk. Stiffly, I walked toward the man who was just getting out of the car. He closed the door and then he turned to me and smiled.

"Congratulations," he said in a deep voice.

"Thank you so much," I replied. I glanced at the car and then over my shoulder at Helen and Mike. I shook my head slowly. "I don't even know what to say," I said. "Thank you."

"No Anne Rose, thank you. Look, baby, look behind you. Look what you've done." Helen wailed after she said that. She let out a loud cry, and Mike held her to his chest.

My heart was beating quickly at the sight of her emotion, but I didn't know why or what was going on. Mike's face crumpled as well, and he gestured behind me, pointing. I turned to face the car salesman. I was about to give him a helpless expression with a shrug since I wasn't sure why my grandparents were both crying uncontrollably.

But when I turned, the man took off his sunglasses, and I stared into a pair of green eyes.

They were my eyes.

It hit me all at once.

My father, whom I had never met, was standing right in front of me. That moment, with us staring into each other's green eyes—I didn't know what he was thinking—but I was just lost.

I was lost in the moment.

I was somehow able to think of nothing and everything all at once. I was speechless and I had sporadic thoughts those silent, stunned seconds. I didn't know if the BMW was really mine or if it was just part of a plan to…

He tentatively, stiffly opened his arms for a hug, and I heard Helen wail again as I walked into them. A massive wave of chills hit my body as we embraced. My father wrapped his arms around me and it was just too much. We both began crying the instant we embraced. He shook with it, which made me cry even harder.

Helen and Mike came up to us, putting hands on our backs, and all of us crying and blubbering in a huddle between two cars. Helen let out uncontrollable wails, and the two men moved, urging her next to me. I let go of Michael with one arm, just enough to hold onto Helen. She took in several gasping breaths, trying to stop crying and get herself together as she looked at us.

"I can't believe it," she said, looking back and forth from one of us to the other. "You did this," she said, looking at me while wiping at her face. "You did this for us, Anne Rose. And I could never thank you enough. Michael and his father spent all morning and afternoon togeth…." Her voice went higher and higher as she spoke and eventually, it was too hard for her to continue the sentence, and she trailed off. She gasped. "Michael and I haven't got to see each other in..."

Mike did the same thing. He tried to take over where Helen left off and he couldn't do it either. He took a minute to get himself together, which was fine with all of us because we were all overwhelmed, anyway.

"I hadn't seen my son in far too long," Mike said. "Not since he became an old man," he added, causing us all, including Michael, to laugh.

"I thank you for letting me come here today," Michael said softly, looking at me but not quite making eye contact. He was tight-jawed and fighting off tears. "My mom knew I'd been selling these cars, so she called me last week, and, well, one thing led to another, and I ended up connecting with Dad, too." He paused and took an emotion-filled breath.

I glanced at him and I could hardly believe how his mouth moved. He was older and he looked different, but our mouths twisted and turned in the same way when we spoke. It wasn't just our eyes. I looked so much like this man.

"I have done a lot of..." He paused again and cleared his throat. "I've made so many mistakes in my life. Too many to count. I've done more bad than good. Honestly, Anne Rose, you're the best thing I think I've accomplished, and I've had almost nothing to do with you."

"Yes, you did. Look at you two. She looks just like you."

"Thank you, Mom, but I'm talking about raising her. I had nothing to do with the way she turned out."

"Well, we've all got some startin' over to do, son," Helen said.

"Some debts to pay, too," Michael said, looking down, acting ashamed.

"Not to me," I said, seeing how bad he felt. "I have a good life. I have a family in Houston, and now I'm here, and you're here, and you guys are standing here, touching each other..." I looked at all three of them one by one, all of us had been crying, and Helen still actively was.

"You guys may have things to talk about, debts that need to be paid, or other things you feel like you need to forgive, but don't factor me into that. As far as I'm concerned, all is forgiven. The choices that we've made up until this point don't have to stop us from going forward. You guys can just choose to forgive and forget." I looked at Michael. "I know they would love that," I said, speaking for Helen and Mike.

Helen continued to sob on Mike's shoulder. "I would too," Michael agreed, looking at his mom.

We all stood there in a loose huddle. Michael had a hand on me and one on his mother, and Mike standing there with his arm around Helen's back.

"You should see that daughter of yours cook," Mike said, trying to say something to get us to stop standing there crying.

"I was hearing about that," Michael agreed, nodding, stepping back. "I guess there's already some special sauce named after you or something."

"Oh, you have to taste it, Michael," Helen said. "The whole dish is excellent. She put sesame oil in that sauce. That's what puts it over the top. Your father never uses sesame oil. Not until now. I think we ordered a gallon of it yesterday."

Michael nodded and smiled shyly. "I heard you graduated with some honors, too," he added. He seemed proud of me, but he had a certain level of meekness or even apology to his countenance. He glanced down a lot.

We all just stood there for a few moments, making small talk to get out of the emotional mode. I could tell that all of them felt bad for their mistakes. I could feel it radiating off of them. And it was out of sheer wanting them to feel better and not at all because I truly cared that I said, "So, is the car seriously mine?"

They all laughed at that. "Yes, my dear!" Helen said. "I hope you don't think we would trick you with that car."

"That would be a pretty cruel trick," Michael added.

I smiled at him after glancing at the car like I loved it, and he tossed me the keys. We were standing close to each other, so the toss was a little bit of a surprise, but I reached out and snagged the keys out of the air.

"Whoa, good catch," Michael said, smiling and looking impressed. I could tell he really liked me which made me feel like crying again. I held it back.

He moved and went to open the driver's door for me. I could see inside because it was a convertible and the top was down. It was a gorgeous shimmering dark blue with tan interior. I could not believe this car was mine. It was immaculate. It was the best car I had ever seen.

"It's a standard," I said. I looked at Michael.

"I know."

"How'd you know I could drive that?" I asked, since none of my friends knew how. My mother didn't even know how. My dad had been the one to teach me. He loved standards and always wanted me to have one.

"I talked to your mom and Kyle."

"You did?" I asked, no longer paying attention to the car.

"Yeah, I mean, I knew they knew about me, and Mom wanted me to talk to them before we made some decisions on the car. There was an automatic on the lot, but your dad, Kyle, thought you might like the standard."

"I do, I really do, but… wow, I had no idea you did all that."

"I met with him and your mother earlier this week," Michael said. "We had lunch together," he nudged his chin toward his parents. "Mom and Dad thought it'd be a good idea to talk to them about the car before they pulled the trigger."

"I talked to Mom several times this week, and she didn't say a thing."

"Because it was a surprise," Helen said, motioning to the car with one hand while she wiped her eyes with the other.

I just stood there and shook my head dazedly. "I was already overwhelmed when you showed me the menu!" I said to her. "And now all this... the car... and him!" I pointed with my thumb at their son, which made everyone laugh. "Seriously," I said, still smiling. "I don't know what to say besides thank you. I can't even believe this is real. I hate to accept this car. The menu... and just... everything else you've done—I don't feel like I can accept the car. It's too much."

I looked at Michael with a reluctant expression when I said that, and he shrugged and gestured to his parents.

"We've already been through all this with your mother," Helen said. "She said the same thing and she said you would say it, too. But Mike and I want to do it. You breathed new life into this restaurant and obviously into us. You changed everything for us, Anne Rose. You're a good girl and we want you to have it. This car is not even enough for how much we feel like we owe you." She smiled and tilted her chin at me. "Why don't you take it for a quick spin?"

she added. "You and Michael go together. We'll stand here and hold your spot."

Chapter 14

I sat in the car and Michael closed the door, which was a surreal experience. The three of them were standing nearby, and they moved so they could get a good view of me once I was seated.

"The controls to adjust the seat are down and on your left," Michael said. "I tried to adjust everything to what I thought would be pretty close to your size while I was waiting for you to come out."

"Thank you," I said. I adjusted in my seat, feeling like I was in the nicest luxury automobile that had ever been made. It seriously might have been. My heart pounded as my eyes scanned the interior.

"Take it for a spin!" Helen said.

She was in the best mood ever.

I put my hand on the gearshift and glanced up at Michael. "You want to ride with me?" I asked.

"Yes, he does. Go, Michael," she said, pushing his shoulder.

And within a minute, I was driving down Seawall Boulevard in a gorgeous convertible with the wind in my hair. "This is un-believable," I said, turning to him at the first traffic light we came to.

"I'm glad you like it," he said.

He was wearing his sunglasses again, and I dug in my purse to find mine. The sun was at our back, but it was bright out. I grinned at him after I put on my glasses, and he sank into his seat with a smile.

"It's got a good sound system, too," he said. "Top of the line speakers with two ten-inch subs and an upgraded amp. I was able to get my manager to throw those in."

"Thank you," I said.

We drove for a mile or so before I turned to make the block and head back to the restaurant. I got stuck at a couple more lights, and each time, Michael showed me something about the car. He was gentle and friendly, and my heart ached because I could feel the regret emanating off of him.

I smiled a lot because I wanted him to know that everything was okay and that I just wanted us all to get along.

"There's a three-year, bumper-to-bumper," he said, breaking the silence while I was in thought. "And I'll talk to Mom about extending it once that time comes, if you're still driving it."

"Oh, goodness, it's so nice, I can't imagine I wouldn't be." I gazed at the dash and wondered why something this nice even needed a warranty.

The light turned green and I drove toward the restaurant. I felt like I was in a dream. And that sensation only intensified when I spotted Will's truck in front of me. I knew it was him because it had two small stickers on the back window—one was from the hardware store and the other was from the boxing gym.

Will was coming to dinner.

He was on his way—headed toward the restaurant.

"I'd love to hear some radio," I said, instantly saying something to distract Michael so that he didn't glance up and see the truck.

He started to mess with the stereo as I sped up and pulled to Will's left side.

"It's got some pick-up, huh?" he said, feeling me push the gas. I could hear the smile in his voice, but I was too distracted.

"Yes, sir," I said, doing my best to stay calm but catch up to Will. I hated to put Michael between Will and me, but I had no choice since Will was driving in the right lane. I drove as carefully as I could, but it was a new car and I was completely frazzled. I did my best to be safe as I thought about how to get Will's attention.

"I'm sorry, but I know this guy, hang on," I said.

I honked the horn right after I said that to Michael. Thankfully, Will was driving with his window down and he heard me. I saw him glance at me from his truck, and I yelled and pointed.

"Pull over!" I yelled. "Hey, Will! Pull into the hotel!" I yelled.

He slowed down, and I took the opportunity to get in the lane in front of him and guide him into the hotel. I was shaken, and I didn't say anything to Michael. I parked in a spot that had nothing available next to it, sandwiching my new convertible in between a van and a big truck.

"I'm sorry," I said, getting out in a hurry. "Wait right here for just a second. I just needed to tell this guy something real quick. Sorry, I'll be right back."

I was speaking quickly and moving at the same time. *Had I just called Will this guy?* Will found a parking spot several places down and was getting out of his truck when I made my way over there.

"What is happening?" he asked. He had the most adorable smile I had ever seen, and I wanted go to him like normal. But I was too nervous for that. I was so overwhelmed with meeting Michael that I hadn't considered what to do about Will tonight. I hugged him while I thought for a second.

"I got a new car," I said, pulling back so I could look at him while I spoke. I knew he could tell something was wrong. His dark brown eyes searched my face. "Helen and Mike bought me that car. First, they did this menu thing where they put one of my dishes on their regular dinner menu, can you believe that?"

"No."

"And then we walked outside and there was that car. It's brand new. And the craziest thing was that *Michael* delivered it. Their son, Michael. My dad. He's a car salesman. They bought it from him. He was here when I got here. He drove it up to me."

"What?" Will asked, glancing that way.

I was speaking quickly and it was a bunch of crazy news so I felt bad. "Michael," I said. "My biological dad. He's here."

"That's him with you in the car?" Will asked, whispering with wide eyes. His eyes shifted that way again, but we couldn't see Michael from where we were standing.

"Yes," I whispered dramatically. I stared up at him. "I misssss youuuu," I moaned.

"I miss you toooo," he said, moaning like me.

It had only been five days, but it felt like forever. I stared into his eyes.

"I love you," I said weakly.

"I love you, too, what's wrong?" he asked.

I tried to think of how I wanted to say it.

"I love you the most, Will, you're the most important to me. So, if this hurts you, you need to tell me. But can we possibly think about making the introduction another night? I am overwhelmed with Michael being here. I did not expect this at all. We were standing outside the restaurant, crying our eyes out before we got in the car just now. I just met him like eight minutes ago. I obviously had no idea he would be here when I planned all this. And you can still come if you want because, like I said, you're the most important to me, but—"

Will reached out to hug me. "Anne Rose, baby, stop worrying about me. I just want to make you happy. I am totally fine not going tonight."

I let out a sigh and hugged him. "I'm sorry. I don't know what else to do. I feel like this Michael thing is going to need all of my attention tonight, but I'm torn because you matter the most to me," I said.

Will wrapped me tightly in his arms. "You matter the most to me, too," he said. "Go do what you need to do and come over to my place afterward."

"What time?" I asked.

"Whenever you get done," he said. "Don't worry about it."

"I am worried about it," I said. "I miss you."

"I miss you, too," he said.

"I want you," I said, leaning into him, and pouting a little.

"I want you, too," he repeated.

"Can I meet you at like eight-thirty?" I asked.

"Yes."

"Where?" I asked.

"Just come to Tara and Trey's. They invited me to stop by for dinner before they knew you were coming in tonight. I'll just go by there. Did you say they put one of your dishes on the menu?"

"Yes. Tacos. Guiltless snapper tacos. Isn't that crazy? There was even a note talking about this sauce I made to go with it. And then the car, and then Michael. I feel like I'm in a dream right now. Are you even standing here?"

I reached up and touched the side of Will's face. I rubbed my fingertips along his skin, checking to see if he was really there, and he smiled. His cheeks shifted as he moved. He had a little dimple on one side, and I ached to kiss it. I did. I leaned upward and kissed his cheek. He wasn't always clean-shaven, but tonight he was. He was dressed nicely, too, looking handsome for me. It completely broke my heart to ask him to leave, but I was already short-circuiting with all of the surprises tonight.

"Go do your thing," he said, urging me along. "I'll see you tonight."

"Are you sure?" I said.

"Yes, of course. And I'm happy you're seeing Michael. Do you feel okay about it? Are you comfortable? Is he nice and everything?"

"Yeah, I just met him but yes, thank you, he is being very nice."

"Good. And congratulations on the car. That thing is awesome."

"Do you want to drive it tonight?" I asked with a smile.

He grinned confidently. "I assumed I would."

"You can," I said, getting close and flirting with him.

"I will," he said.

"We could just go park somewhere and look at the stars. There's no top."

"I saw that," he said with a smile.

I honestly loved this man, and I wanted to make sure he was okay right now. I was happy about the car and about my newfound family and their reconciliation with each other, but Will was everything. At that moment, I felt like I wanted to fast-forward my evening three hours and find myself in his arms again.

"I'll see you at Tara's at eight-thirty," he said.

"Okay," I replied, even though it broke my heart.

"Okay," Will agreed easily.

I reached up and kissed his cheek. "I'll see you soon," I said, giving him a squeeze.

I jogged to the spot five places down where my car was parked. It was a full parking lot, and I was thankful for the cover of all the cars. Michael was staring straight ahead, not seeming at all nosy about what I was doing. I didn't say anything to him until I got into the car.

"Thank you for waiting," I said when I sat in the driver's seat.

"No problem," he said. "I'm glad you saw your friend."

I loved Will so much that it was impossible for me to let that slip past without correcting him. "He's my boyfriend, actually," I said.

"Oh really?"

"Yeah. Big time."

"Does he live in Galveston?"

"Yes sir."

"Is he coming to eat with us tonight?" Michael asked.

"I... I thought about it, but no, h-he can't."

"What's his name?" Michael asked.

My heart dropped because I could feel that Michael was onto something.

"Will Castro," I said.

"Billy's boy?"

"Yes sir." I was shaking on the inside, but I tried to keep my voice calm and steady.

Michael let out a long, defeated sigh.

"What is it?" I said.

"It's, I'm, it's, uhhhh, I saw that sticker on the back of his truck. King's Hardware. It's just that name." He took another long, thoughtful breath. "Laney King. I haven't even said that name out loud in almost twenty years, goodness. I'm sorry. I just had a long string of regrets in my life, and how I treated Laney was the one that started it all off."

"I knew there was some history or whatever between the families, but Will, he doesn't care about any of that. I'm pretty sure you don't even care about Laney and them anymore."

"I'm pretty sure I'll never love anyone else in my whole life, but—"

"Oh, gosh, I am so sorry," I said.

"No, no, it's not... none of this is your fault. It's just crazy seeing that name and then you pulled him over. I was just praying it wasn't her kid. That would be too much."

He took another deep breath. He wasn't trying to be dramatic. He honestly looked like he was keeping it together as much as he could. I thought of Laney and her twins, Jenny and Josh, and how they were really close to Will and at all of his family get-togethers.

"I actually don't care that you're seeing him, but I wouldn't tell Mom," Michael said.

"What? Sir?"

"Does Mom know you're seeing that boy?"

"No sir. Helen? She knows I have a boyfriend who lives here, but she—I was going to introduce them."

"It's up to you, but I wouldn't tell her," he said.

Chapter 15

I left the restaurant at 8:34pm.

I was already late, and it would take me eight more minutes to get to Tara's. I had done my absolute best to get out of there and on my way to Will on time, but the Elliots had a lot of ground to cover tonight, and the time had passed in a blur. As it stood, I already felt like I was skipping-out too early.

Megan came with her husband. They had two kids, but both of them were grown and out of the house, and neither of them came to dinner. The six of us sat at a table in the back and talked continually through dinner. Most of the conversation revolved around me because, to them, I signified a new beginning, something else to cling to and talk about besides the past.

Michael didn't flinch when we brought up my boyfriend. He even asked me a few vague questions about Will. Megan's husband left when I did, but the others all stayed at the restaurant. They had a lot to catch up on without me, but they were putting it off somewhat while Darren and I were there.

I already had plans to spend the night in their guesthouse and to wake up to make food in the morning like we always did on Saturday. In a change of events, however, Michael had decided to stay the night as well. The new plan was that he would spend the night in the main house, in his old bedroom, and we would wake up and cook together in the morning. It worked out because we had already planned on cooking at the house rather than worrying about going to the restaurant.

It had been an unbelievable evening. We sat around that table in the back of their restaurant, interacting with Michael after what had been decades. It was busy in there, and Mister Elliot was famous for socializing with his customers, so they put a divider in front of our table, and no one besides our severs came up to us.

There were tears and there was forgiveness and reconciliation, and not a single person brought up past hurts or anything else negative that would cause confrontation. But it had been over twenty years, and there were a few awkward moments. Honestly, it was a good thing I was there. I fell accidently into the role of mediator even though I barely knew Megan and didn't know Michael at all.

My mind was spinning, and I was in a hurry to get to Will.

I hated being late to get to him. If my life in the last few hours hadn't been so packed full of unbelievable circumstances, I would have made it on time. But as it stood, it was an absolute miracle that I was here even close to time.

It was 8:43 when I parked in front of Tara's place on Bank Street. It was a safe neighborhood and I didn't even worry about putting the top up. I had already closed the door and was about to head inside when I heard my name.

"Hey Anne Rose!" It was Tara speaking, I looked up and could see her standing at the second story window.

"Hey! So sorry I'm late."

"Don't worry. Will knew you had something with your family. He's on his way down now. Hey, nice car. Will said he gets to go on a drive first, but I want you to take me tomorrow or some other time."

"I'd love to!" I said.

"Are you spending the night in Galveston?" she asked.

"Yeah."

"Maybe tomorrow then," she said.

"Of course!"

"Hey, Anne Rose!" her husband, Trey, called to me as he came to the window.

I smiled because it was fun talking to them from below. "Hey Trey."

"Cool car."

"Thanks. I just got it. It's my second time to drive it."

"Will was telling us that," Trey said. "BMW?"

"Yeah," I said.

"What model?" he asked.

But by this time, Will had come out of the door and I got distracted. He crossed the sidewalk, and made it to me in what seemed like two seconds. He didn't stop when he got next to me, either. He took me into his arms, causing me to let out a little yelp and laugh before he set me back on my feet.

"It's a three... twenty... eight... i," I said, laughing as Will set me down, causing my voice to shake.

"Niiiice!" Trey said. "Y'all have fun!" he added, turning to look at his wife.

"Yeah, bye, y'all have fun," Tara said.

"I'm gonna go drive this thing," Will said to his sister. "We'll be back in a little while to get my truck."

"Okay, but come upstairs before you leave," she said. "I have Anne Rose's graduation card up here."

"Okay, we'll be back in a little while."

"If it's past ten, just come tomorrow. Nick's getting tired."

"Sounds good," Will said. "Thanks for dinner."

"You're welcome. Love y'all. Congratulations on graduating, Anne Rose... and the car!"

"Thank you," I said, waving. I came really close to adding, "Love you too," but I didn't say it.

"Bye, love you," Will said.

Tara waved again as she closed the window, giving us privacy. Will still had me in his arms from when he first came outside. He had never let me go. I was nervous about seeing him, and hollering at his family from upstairs had distracted me in a good way.

"Hi," I said, feeling more confident after talking to them.

"Hi, my love."

He leaned in and kissed me on the cheek, right next to my mouth, and I let out a little sound of approval. He did it again, same spot, and I let out a similar short sound. I had been aching to see him, touch him. I did not take for granted the feel of his muscles as he held me.

"I'm late," I said in a regretful tone.

"You had a few things to deal with over there," he said. His countenance was full of patience and forgiveness, and I clung to him.

"Michael's staying the night," I said.

"Tonight? Where? At his parents'?"

"Yes. It's crazy. It's been twenty years, and now he's having a sleepover."

We heard someone yell from down the street. They weren't yelling at us, but the sound broke our trance and Will stuck his hand out.

"Come on. Hand me your keys, and we'll go somewhere else where we can talk."

Within minutes, we were parked at the beach. It was a public area along the seawall, but there weren't many people out there at this time of night, so we easily found a secluded spot. We hadn't been able to talk while we were driving with the top down, so he turned to me as soon as we parked and he turned off the engine.

"Do you want to walk or stay in here?" he asked.

"I wouldn't mind a walk," I said. "But I think we should put the top up."

He nodded. "We definitely should, if we're going for a walk."

It took us about five minutes to figure out the top and get the car locked up. Michael had shown me briefly how to do it, but I was worried about making sure everything was locked into place.

Will and I left our shoes in my car and took off on a walk down the beach.

"So, what a night, huh?" Will asked, smiling at me as he wrapped his arm around my shoulders.

I glanced up at him, and because he was looking straight ahead, I got a view of the bottom of his jaw. I could see the side of his face, and I loved him so much my heart felt like it might come to pieces just from looking at him.

"I have to get all this settled," I said, shaking my head. "I was helping that family heal from all of their own stuff tonight, and the whole time, I just kept thinking... none of this even matters if they won't accept Will."

"It does," he said. "It matters."

"Yeah, but if they make me choose between them and you, I'm choosing—"

"But it hasn't come to that," Will said before I could finish.

"I know, but it's always in the back of my mind that it will. I mean, that's the logical thing, right, is that they're going to freak out and force me to choose between you guys, and then I'm going to choose you. I'd rather just know right now if they can handle it or not. I should have let you come to the restaurant tonight. I was just so worried about Michael reuniting with his parents that I... but I don't even want to drive this car if I'm going end up having to give it back. So, I don't know what to do."

Will could tell by my ramblings that I was upset. "Just listen," he said patiently. "Give me a week. Let's plan to get both sides together next Saturday morning. I'll talk to everyone at once. You might as well see if you can get Michael to come back. Whoever you feel like. You can even invite your mom and dad if you want."

"I don't think they need to be here," I said. "They really don't have anything to do with this. I'm more worried about Laney and Abby—your side. I know they're going to take it a little differently than my parents would. I'm not looking forward to having Laney and Michael in a room at the same time, but I also don't want any misunderstandings."

"And when we talk to everyone, what do you think we should say?" he asked.

"I just want them all to know who you are and who I am and that we like each other. I just want them all to know that. I would still want to be with you if they object, but we need to let them know. I can't keep hiding it. Before you said that thing about waiting a week, I was planning on telling them tomorrow morning at breakfast. At least my side. I had my heart set on them meeting you earlier tonight, and I hate it that they don't know. Especially now, with the car. Michael will be there with us, and that way, if they can't accept it, he can take the car back with him—just drive it back to Houston tomorrow. I still have my Honda."

"Don't worry about the car," Will said. "If you want to do it tomorrow, we'll do it tomorrow. Everything's going to be okay. We'll get everyone together at the same time, that way they have to look at each other. We still have to figure out where to have them meet, though. My family isn't going to want to go to the restaurant, and your family won't go to the hardware store or the gym."

"We need a neutral location," I said. "What about your apartment? You could invite your family over, and I could show up with mine."

"You know they'll feel ambushed, right?"

"Which ones?"

"Everyone," he said.

I groaned, knowing he was right.

"Plus, I don't know how many I can get from my side on such short notice."

I thought about it for a minute.

"Okay, I have an idea. Let's do it at the Elliots' house for breakfast. I'll tell them I want them to meet my boyfriend and his family. My crew will already be there, and you can bring your family to us. If you can't get them all, maybe you can at least get your mom and your aunts."

Will nodded thoughtfully. "They won't know where we're going until we get there, and by then I'll be able to talk them into hearing me out."

"Yeah, this'll be perfect. They have a really nice patio out back, and I'll tell them that you're bringing your family to introduce them. That way they'll know to expect company, they just won't know who it is until you guys show up. Michael will. But I don't think he'll say anything. He's really easygoing."

"I think it's a good plan," Will said with a smile. I could tell he thought I was cute.

"What?" I said.

"You called me your boyfriend." He was teasing me, and I got embarrassed enough that I let out a noise and ran away from him on the beach. He knew I didn't mind him teasing me. I acted more embarrassed than I was, and it was fun for me to pretend I wanted to get away.

Will gave chase, and he easily caught up to me, hugging me and taking me captive in his arms. My back was now to his chest and he leaned down and put his face near the side of my face and neck. I reached up and put my hand on the back of his head. He had his hands gently wrapped around my stomach, and my blood turned warm.

"I want you to tell them I'm your boyfriend," he said. "I was just messing with you. I'd be sad if you don't call me that."

He kissed my neck, and my hand flexed on the back of his head, my fingertips moving through his hair. I was happy we had set a time for our families to meet, and I was happy that it was going to be tomorrow.

"Thank you for understanding everything, Will. I know it's a complicated situation, and I'm sorry we have to deal with it as part of our... story."

He adjusted me and we began to walk slowly up the shore. "It's not complicated," he said.

Will was practical and easygoing, and I wanted to believe him, but I glanced at him with a look of disbelief.

He smiled. "It's not. We can't help who our parents are. All the stuff is old. They've all moved on and gotten older. We'll tell them we love each other and they'll be fine with it."

"You promise?" I asked.

Will looked right at me and smiled thoughtfully. "I pretty-much promise," he said. "No, I take that back. I promise. I'm going to see to it. Everything's going to be fine."

Chapter 16

Will

The following morning

Will had a whole speech planned. He had to come up with a way to make them all get along. There was just no other option but to do that. He knew it would be left up to him to change everyone's attitude about this relationship.

Will had promised Anne Rose that he would take care of it and that everything would be okay, and he meant to stay true to that promise. He hardly slept that night because of how seriously he was taking that promise.

He stayed with Anne Rose until midnight and then he was up until 2am, thinking about what he'd say to everyone in the morning. At first, he thought he'd do some freestyling, but eventually he came up with some points he wanted to make.

He was going to start off by thanking them for being there and explaining the fact that he and Anne Rose been seeing each other for months already.

He was going to talk about Romeo and Juliet. He would say, *gone are the days of Romeo and Juliet*, and he would explain why, as reasonable God-fearing adults, they should forgive each other for past offenses and move forward.

He knew he could rely on his family to be patient and let him explain once they got there, and he knew what he would say. But now that it was time for it to all go down, Will was extremely nervous.

He was shaking. The plan was for the family to meet him at his parents' house and follow Will to a different location. He didn't tell them they were going anywhere. He just told them to meet at his parents' house thirty minutes before they were supposed to be at the Eilliots'.

Last night, Will and Anne Rose had made sure the whole family was invited. They were so determined to make this day happen, that they went straight to Tara's after they had the conversation on the beach. They went inside and invited Tara and Trey to a family meeting. (Will told them he was just trying to get the family together, but it was obvious that Tara and Trey thought he and Anne Rose were getting engaged.)

They called and invited everyone in his family that might have an objection to him being with Michael's daughter. He assumed that some wouldn't be able to be there on such short notice, but every single person he invited said they'd come.

The guest list was as follows:
Tess

Billy
Trey
Tara (little Nickel)
Aunt Abby
Uncle Daniel
Evan
Izzy
Aunt Laney (yikes)
Uncle James (double-yikes)
Josh
Jenny

Jenny's boyfriend also came because he was at their house when they left.

They caravanned in four cars and followed Will to the neighborhood where the Elliots lived. His mom and dad rode with him, and they were both looking at him like he was crazy when he pulled up in front of their house. It was an unmistakable home where the Elliots had lived for decades.

Will's parents didn't even consider that they might be going to a neighbor's house. They were concentrating on the Elliots' place as soon as they turned on that street.

Will parked and got out to stand by his truck. Others behind him had parked and were beginning to open car doors. He could see their confused faces as they stepped out. "Just come out here. Everyone get your things and let me talk to you guys for a minute."

"We could have talked at home!" It was Aunt Laney who said it. She was trying to sound playful, but Will knew she was the one who would likely be most affected by being there, and he glanced at her with a sympathetic expression. She was standing up, but she hadn't moved away from her car.

"I know, Aunt Laney. Just please hear me out."

She finally closed the door and came closer to Will who was standing on the sidewalk.

She was wearing a serious expression, which was saying a lot. In this moment, Will realized that the women in his family smiled all the time. He realized it because they were currently not smiling, and he thought about how different they all looked.

"Aunt Laney, I want you to be here. I want all of you here. Please just take a minute and hear what I have to say," Will said.

"What are you doing, Will?" James asked.

"He said he has something to say," Josh said.

"What do you have to say?" James asked.

"Yeah, Will, does it have to do with the Elliots?" Jenny asked.

"Yes, it does," Will said. "But it's not bad. It's good. Please. Just all of you, trust me. Come with me. It's around back. Just follow me for a minute."

Anne Rose had already told Will where to go and that she would meet him on the side of the house to let them into the gate at this exact time.

The Castros, Kings, and the Grahams all trusted and loved Will, so they followed him without asking any more questions about it. There were, however, a few shared glances behind his back as he led the way up their driveway and toward the side of the house.

Will was happy to lay eyes on Anne Rose, but he quickly noticed that her expression was apologetic, and a few steps behind her was the not-so-happy Helen Elliot.

"I *do not* think so!" she said. "I'm not having this mob on my lawn. I'm pressing charges on all of you if you come any farther on my property!" She looked at Anne Rose with a stern expression. "How could you even think about doing this with your father here?" Helen shook her head at Anne Rose like she was disappointed in her, and Will thought he might just burst into flames.

He went to Anne Rose. They had been standing apart, but she saw Will moving toward her, and she came his way, the two of them meeting in the middle of the two sides. She latched onto him, and he prayed to God for the ability to turn this situation around.

He saw Mike and his son, Michael Junior, coming out of the house using a side door. His heart hammered, and he wondered if it was too late to say never mind to this whole conversation.

"What's this all about?" Mike asked, yelling when he made it out onto the porch. Michael was there with his dad, and Will could hear his own family reacting to seeing them both. The two of them walked the few feet away from the door and met up with Helen on the driveway.

The families were standing twenty feet from each other with the young couple sandwiched in the middle. Anne Rose and Will were holding onto each other. They positioned themselves where she was mostly looking at her family and he was mostly looking at his.

Will turned to look at Helen, giving her a beseeching smile. "My name's Will Castro." He was about to add that he was Anne Rose's boyfriend, but that was probably obvious by the way she was holding him.

Anne Rose straightened resolutely when Will started talking. She wanted Helen to know that she wanted Will and his family to be there. She stood beside him, holding on to his arm lightly. Will touched her lower back, and she leaned into it. He took three steps forward and then turned around with Anne Rose in his grasp. Now they were positioned like more of a triangle instead of right between two opposing sides. This way, they could see everyone.

He kept talking quickly, though, not giving anyone time to protest or question what was going on. "I need three minutes of your time," Will said. He looked at Helen. "Is there any chance we can take this somewhere besides the driveway."

She paused and it was obvious she was thinking about agreeing for Anne Rose's sake, but she shook her head, stubbornly refusing. "You can say what you need to say out here."

Will let Helen's refusal roll off his back and he began speaking without missing a beat. He was a nervous wreck, but there was no way he was backing down. The energy in the air was charged, and both Will and Anne Rose looked back and forth between the two sides, almost as if they were making sure a fight didn't break out.

"Okay," Will said. "Anne Rose and I have spent a lot of time together in the past six months. Most of you have known that, but none of you have known the full scope of things. Anne Rose was raised in Houston by the Kennedy family and recently found out that Michael Elliot was her biological father."

"She would have known a lot sooner if I had anything to do with it," Helen blurted.

"Anne Rose loves you guys," Will said, looking at Helen. "She was genuinely excited last night, and it had nothing to do with the car. She loves you. She loves it that Michael came, and she loves it that you're reconnecting. Plus, she loves the restaurant." He paused and looked around and everyone. "But she loves me, too."

He was just about to go into the whole Romeo and Juliet spiel that he thought of last night. It was on the tip of his tongue, and he was just about to deliver his first sentence about Romeo and Juliet being outdated and irrelevant.

Gone are the days of Romeo and Juliet... his opening line got stuck in his mind and wouldn't come out of his mouth.

He looked around not knowing what to say.

And for some reason, he took notice that his dad had on a gold chain with a cross. He glanced at Helen who was also wearing a cross necklace. Laney's T-shirt said *blessed* on it, and Will mentally shifted gears without even thinking about it.

Jesus was the common ground.

Will cleared his throat.

"I went to church camp when I was in eighth grade, and this guy, this guest speaker, told this story about a little boy in London, England who watched a parade with his grandfather. They were at a church, and they stood in an upstairs window to view a parade as it passed by on the street below. *'That's the royal army'*, the grandfather said. *'The soldiers in the red coats, those are the Queen's soldiers'*. But the boy didn't see any soldiers in red coats, and he told his grandfather so. He only saw the soldiers in white coats. All of them had on white coats. *'The ones right here below us'*, the grandfather said, pointing them out again. But the boy only saw soldiers in white. The grandfather looked all around and realized that there were no soldiers in white. And, taking a step back, he also realized that the boy, being so much shorter than he, had been viewing the parade through a section of red stained glass window. The grandfather ducked, looking again at the soldiers, this time from the boy's vantagepoint, through the stained glass. Indeed, with this red filter, the soldiers' coats were white. It wasn't that the soldiers had *actually* changed from red to white. It was that they were being viewed through a filter, and the filter changed how they appeared."

Will used his hand to indicate that there was an imaginary piece of glass in front of himself. Everyone was watching him, listening to him.

"So, the guy at camp was saying how Jesus, and that amazing thing He did by sacrificing Himself, was the filter that God is able to see us through. It's not that we're without sin... it's just that through the filter, we appear that way. Our red coats look to be white."

Will looked around, and took a deep breath. He was out of words and fully relying on God and intuition to finish what he was saying. He hadn't planned on saying any of this. He hadn't thought of that story in years. He made eye contact with Helen, who was slightly less angry looking now.

"What I'm asking you guys to do in this moment is similar to that. Anne Rose and I love each other. We are what we are. We're staying together. She is Michael's blood daughter, and she loves the Elliots. I obviously love my family very much, too." He glanced back-and-forth to each family. "We're asking you guys to see the Elliots through me. And we're asking you guys to see my family through Anne Rose. If you can't bring yourselves to just

160

forgive each other and start over on your own, try looking at each other through us. Know that we are going to be together. We've figured that out and planned it out, and that's what's going to happen. And we'd love for you guys to just be able to start over and see each other as blameless for our sakes. Please."

It was silent for a few seconds but Michael, Anne Rose's dad was the first to speak up. Will thought it would be someone from his side, but it was Michael.

"Well, I'm batting a thousand this weekend on new beginnings, so I honestly don't have a problem with any of this."

Anne Rose had told Will that Michael recognized his truck when they pulled over at the hotel the night before. Michael had an evening to let this news digest. He was wearing a calm, easy smile.

"Well, goodness, Will," Laney said. "You know none of us are going to be able to say anything after that whole Jesus speech."

Multiple people laughed at her comment, including Will and Anne Rose.

"I wasn't even planning on saying that," he said. "I was going to talk about Romeo and Juliet."

That made more people laugh.

"What about all this food?" Michael had been the one to ask the question, but he did it quietly enough that Will's family didn't hear.

Will didn't have hopes that Helen would agree to breakfast, but her expression had softened, and he was pretty sure she wasn't going to call the police on them.

"Listen," Helen said, getting everyone's attention. "My nerves are already shot this weekend, anyway. Mike's too. So, I don't see why we should let all this food go to waste. Anne Rose told us you had a big group coming, and we've got a ton of food in here."

Chapter 17

Anne Rose

I originally hoped that Will's family would stay for breakfast, otherwise I wouldn't have urged us to prepare so much. However, seeing Helen's initial reaction to them being there was eye-opening, and I didn't have much hope that there would be any quality time spent together after the conversation in the driveway.

At first, it felt like the two of us were standing in the driveway surrounded by a bunch of people with resentment and frustration aimed at us. But Will turned it around. He spoke some words and changed their minds. He gently pointed out that we all need forgiveness. And then Helen asked them to stay, which by the time it happened, seemed completely unexpected.

Almost everyone stayed. I couldn't believe it, but they did. Laney and James were the only family who left. She came up to me and Will when we were standing next to the Elliots.

"Hey, y'all I'm not going to stay for my husband's sake, so we'll take off with our crew, but thank you for inviting us, and I wanted to say that it's all water under the bridge on our end."

"Yeah, the kids are the bridge in this equation, I guess," Michael said, causing Laney to let out a grateful laugh.

"Yeah, yeah, they are," she said. "I just wanted y'all to know there's no hard feelings, and that the kids have our blessing. We all love Anne Rose. We always say how Will did good when he found her."

She smiled awkwardly, hoping that was enough to say. I could tell she hated to leave but that she knew she couldn't stay. I completely understood, especially after what Michael said about still loving her. She could probably tell he did.

"Thank you," I said, reaching out to hug her. "I understand, and thank you for saying all that."

She gave quick half-hugs to all of the Elliots, exchanging as much sincerity as she could while not causing unnecessary hard feelings to her husband who was standing nearby. James was being kind about everything, wearing a neutral but supportive-looking expression. He and the twins (along with Jenny's boyfriend) converged, spoke to each other, and began to head for the gate. They waved at all of us with smiles and expressions that said there were no hard feelings.

Laney hugged both Will and I and told us she loved us. She said we were good kids and she was happy that we found each other. It was the best possible outcome, and yet it was still edged with the scars of painful memories.

So, Laney and her crew left, but everyone else stayed for breakfast. Will's family talked about me loving to cook, and once we started to eat, they all talked about how delicious the food was. We connected over food, and nothing from the past was brought up.

Will and I both talked a lot. He asked me questions about cooking and restaurant life, and I would do my best to answer them but always get help from the Elliots. Billy loved to cook, too, and all that talk about food got him involved in the conversation.

The Elliots had secretly been fans of Billy during his career, and I could tell they were glad he was at their house. It made me proud that Will's dad was famous. His mom was, too, and Helen ended up asking about Tess's art. We ate and talked, and it was all very cordial and mostly not awkward at all.

And then, a little over an hour later, Will's family packed up to leave. Billy and Tess originally rode with Will, but they hitched a ride back with Tara and Trey so that Will could stay with me. Tara and Trey were on their way to a wedding, and their parents were babysitting Nick since they would be gone all day. It worked out for us that they left together because Will got to stay with me.

Will had gone outside to walk everyone out and say goodbye. It was the first time I was alone with the Elliots, and I was a little intimidated about what they would say.

Helen was at the sink, washing dishes. She was quiet with her back turned toward me.

"Can I help you?" I asked.

"If you want to," she said. "You can rinse those."

I came to stand next to her and began rinsing the plates she had just scrubbed.

"Are we going to be okay? Me and you? Do we need to talk?"

"About what?" she asked without smiling.

"About the fact that I surprised you today. Or the fact that I've been dating Will for months."

She glanced at me. She looked stern. Her mouth was set in a straight line. "Anne Rose, twenty years ago, I might have had a lot to say to you right now. Or I might have not wanted to talk to you at all. I don't know what I would have said. But either way, I'm different now than I was then." She spoke in a dazed tone. "I don't think I have the energy for hurt feelings anymore. As long as you say you want to be in my life, I'm fine with—"

"I do," I said.

"Then, I want to just try to get past all this." She shook her head. "Honestly, seeing those people show up at my house wasn't how I wanted to start my morning. But Billy's boy gave that nice speech, and..." she let out a sigh. "I've wasted too much time being angry with my circumstances instead of just changing them. Reconnecting with Michael this weekend showed me how much time I've wasted. But, no, Anne Rose, if you would have told me a year ago that I'd have my son spending the night in his bedroom one night and then Laney King and her whole crew coming over the next day to tell me that my new granddaughter is in love with one of them, I would have probably called you crazy. But here we are. And when it comes down to it, why be mad? What's there to be mad at, I guess."

"Yeah, that's what I was hoping for," I said. "I knew I needed to tell you about Will, but I just couldn't find the right time. I felt so bad taking that car when you didn't know about him. I needed to get that straight—make sure you didn't want it back when you found out."

"Oh, yeah, Mom and Dad said the car is off the table now that you're with a Castro. I'm supposed to take it back to Houston with me." Michael spoke up from the hallway. He came into the room with us, overhearing our conversation.

My heart dropped a little at his words, and I glanced back at him only to find that he was smiling.

"Michael, don't you tease this poor girl," Helen said.

Michael came up to us, with a smile, and I smiled at him shook my head. "I seriously feel bad about that car," I said to both of them. "It's too much."

"Michael doesn't think it's too much," she said. "He's the one who gets the commission."

"I didn't take a commission on it, Mom. I had Stan write that out of the price."

"He did," Mike agreed, coming into the room behind him.

"You didn't have to do that," Helen said. "We bought it from you to support you."

"Michael and I already talked about it and worked something out," Mike said to his wife. I could tell he wanted to talk about it later, so I cut into the conversation.

"Thank you all for everything this morning," I said.

"Yeah, I wasn't expecting the Kings and Castros to show up on my lawn," Mike said. He was straight-faced, but I could tell he was being lighthearted about it.

"I'm still in shock," Helen said.

She was serious. She washed dishes and seemed dazed and lost in thought, but there was an underlying sense of peace and contentment. It was a difficult interaction, but it had been therapeutic and there was a general sense of relief.

Will knocked on the front door and we all heard it. I moved to go let him in, but Michael was closer to the door and he flinched before I did.

"I'll get it," he said.

I nodded and relaxed next to Helen at the sink, still rinsing. "I love you and I'm thankful you're doing your best to trust people—to be flexible and let people back in."

She thought about my words and then she let out a little humorless laugh. "You'd probably be a lot more mature about all this if you were in my shoes," she said, staring at the dishes.

I leaned into her. "That's not true," I said. "I'm really thankful for the way you guys are handling things."

Mike was standing close enough to us that he heard me say that. Helen glanced at him and they exchanged weary smiles. I was glad they were smiling at all.

I turned to the door as soon as I heard Will come in. It took a few seconds for him and Michael to round the corner to the place where I could see him. They were talking, but it was low enough that I couldn't hear. Will looked my way and gave me a little smile before talking to Michael again. Helen glanced over her shoulder, looking at the two of them for a few long seconds. "He is a handsome boy," she said.

"Which one?" I asked.

"Both of them," she said with a little smile. "I was talking about William. But they're both handsome. And Michael's still my little boy even though he has grey hair." She looked at me. "I guess, if you move to Galveston, he might be coming around once in a while... to see you," she said.

It was the first time she had mentioned me moving there since she found out about Will. I felt relief wash over me that the offer was still open. "I love you guys and I'm definitely still up for moving over here and working at the restaurant if you'll have me."

Helen glanced at me and blinked. Her expression was full of emotion. She wore it all over her face.

"Of course we'll have you, Anne Rose. Neither of our children are interested in the restaurant, and having you around... it's breathing new life into Mike."

"Yeah, and new items on the menu," Mike said.

"Yeah, he's just interested in you for your menu items," Helen said, giving me a wink.

Considering the fact that Mike had kept himself closed off to his own son for years, you'd never believe it, but he was a big softy. Maybe that was why he did close himself off.

"Will said he can get somebody to look at that window for you, Dad," Michael said, coming into the room.

"We work with a lot of contractors," Will said. "And I've been doing some of that myself. I know a lot of good carpenters and craftsmen. I'd be able to introduce you to someone good who'd fix you up and be honest."

"That whole window frame needs repair, and the lavatory in the women's bathrooms," Helen said.

"Yes, ma'am, I bet I know five different guys who could fix you up. Just let me know if I can ever give you some names. They'd be happy to come out and give you a bid."

"A bid from King's Hardware, huh?" she said, shaking her head like she never thought she'd see the day.

I rinsed the last plate and set it to dry on the rack before drying my hands. "Do any of you want to do anything? Go anywhere? The beach, maybe?"

"I have a friend coming to pick me up from Houston," Michael said. "She was supposed to come last night, and I already rescheduled once when I decided to spend the night. She'll be here at two."

"Yeah, and I was thinking about a nap after all this excitement," Helen said, turning from the sink.

"All right, well, I'm going to go out with Will, then," I said. I looked at Michael. "I'm headed back to Houston tonight if you want to ride with me instead of your friend."

He paused and looked at the clock. He hesitated. "I'd actually be fine with that, if you don't mind."

"No," I said. "I'll probably head back around six or seven."

He glanced at the clock. "I bet I can catch her if I call now." And Michael went to the other side of the room to use the phone.

"I'll wait to see if he's riding with me, but either way, I'll come back over here before I head back to Houston," I said to Helen and Mike.

"Sounds good. When are you coming back?" Helen asked.

"Maybe dinner time. But don't worry about cooking. I can just heat up something quick or wait till I get back to Houston.

"I'll just make a salad," Mike said. "You'll need something good and light for the road.

I knew his definition of a salad was a full meal, and that he would spend a lot of time and effort preparing it. But he smiled like he was looking forward to it, and quite frankly I was looking forward to eating whatever he made.

"Can you make one for Will?" I asked.

"He doesn't have to—"

"Sure," Mike said. "I'll have them ready for six o'clock so you can get on the road after dinner."

Chapter 18

Will and I left the Elliots' house a few minutes later. I told them we'd be back in time to visit for a little while before dinner. Will left his truck at their house, and we got into my new car. It still didn't seem real. I watched Will driving it, and I saw the wind in his hair.

He had done it.

He had told our families that we were together, and he talked them into being okay with it.

The cloud of doubt that hung over our relationship was gone.

There were no more secrets.

Will had basically told them to forgive each other for our sakes, and with the way he phrased it, no one could really argue.

I felt elated. If it were possible to bottle this feeling and sell it I would make a zillion dollars.

"Where are we going?" I asked, knowing we left without talking about it.

"My sister is going to that wedding in Bayou Vista all day."

"Yeah, I heard her talking about that. I didn't think you were going."

"I'm not," Will said. "I'm just saying—she's not at home."

"Okay?" I said.

"She's not at home right now, and I wanted to take you over to her house and show you something while we have the place to ourselves."

I laughed, thinking he was joking, but Will didn't laugh back. "For real?" I asked.

"Yes."

"What is it?"

"You'll see."

"Wouldn't Tara be mad?"

"No, not really. She was mad when I found it, but she's over it. She doesn't care if I use it."

"Will, that does not sound like good logic," I said. "If she doesn't want us there, then she might get upset. And I'm ready to not upset anyone anymore."

Will laughed and reached out to hold my hand. My car was a standard, and he was driving in stop and go traffic, so there was no opportunity for him to hold onto me. He did however, take my hand and put it on his own leg. I had been asking about Tara and whether or not she wanted us at her unoccupied house, and then suddenly, I could think of nothing besides the feel of his warm leg through the thin layer of denim.

"I love this car," he said. "I've never driven a convertible before. Not a car, at least. I've driven a couple of jeeps and of course motorcycles and four wheelers and everything. But never just a convertible car."

Will looked sharp in jeans and a light blue short-sleeve button down shirt. The sun was shining down on his dark hair, making him look like a male model at some kind of photoshoot down in Miami.

"What are you thinking about?" he asked, out of nowhere.

"Miami," I said.

He turned to me with a smile. "Miami?"

"Yeah, you look like you're in Miami with your shirt and your hair all shining in the sun."

"Thank you for checking me out so hard," he said with a little smile.

"You're welcome," I said. "I'm happy to. Anytime."

I was in love. There was no doubt about it. I had found the one. At this point, our family connections felt more like a confirmation than a deal breaker.

We only had to drive for a few more minutes to get to Bank Street. Tara and Trey lived on a busy corner, but we easily found a parking place. Will went ahead and closed the top even though it was a pretty day and the car would have probably been fine.

We went into the ballet studio, and Will was disappointed when he found the door open. Jennifer was inside, and she came down the hallway when she heard us come in.

"Oh, hey Will. Hey Anne Rose." She knew we were seeing each other, but she still looked a little surprised to see us together.

"Are there classes right now?" Will asked.

"We're just wrapping up," she said. "Did you need something?"

"Oh, no," Will said. "Anne Rose and I are going to hang out down here for a little while when you're done," he said. "But we'll go over to Carson's while we wait for you guys to finish up. You can lock it up when you leave. I have a key."

"All right," she said. "But we're just back here in the back. You're welcome to use this room."

"That's okay," Will said, not offering any further explanation.

"Are you teaching Anne Rose how to dance?" she asked as she retreated down the hall.

Will smiled. "She's teaching me!" he called back to her.

We walked out of the ballet studio and onto the sidewalk. Will headed across the street and I followed him. "I thought you were going to your sister's apartment," I said. "I feel better that it's the studio. But you probably shouldn't have told Jennifer we were coming back if you didn't want your sister knowing," I said. "She's gonna tell her she saw us there."

Will gave me an easygoing smile as if to say he wasn't worried about it. "I'll tell Tara myself," he said. "It's no big deal. She knows I go in the studio sometimes. She's the one who gave me a key."

Will looked at me as we headed down the sidewalk toward the diner. We would pass his dad's gym on our way there, but we hadn't made it there yet. Will turned to me, walking backwards casually and smiling.

Will and I went to the diner together. We sat at the bar and I remembered that first conversation we had there. I loved him so much it hurt. I was proud of him. I wanted everyone to know we were together. I constantly wanted to touch him because of that. I wanted a jacket that said *Will's Girl* in big letters across the back. I would have seriously worn one of those straight into that diner if I owned one.

We sat at the bar and had a cup of coffee and split a cookie. We talked about everything that had been said that morning, and I laughed when he recounted that helpless feeling he got when he was talking to everyone.

He told the story from his perspective, which was far different than mine.

I told him how confident and sure he sounded, and he got a good kick out of me thinking he had it all together the whole time.

We stayed in the diner for an hour and then made our way back to the ballet studio. No one was there when we got back. The door was locked, and Will opened it with his key.

He reached out for me as he went inside, and I held his hand. He locked the door behind us, and we were suddenly alone in the open studio space.

There were windows everywhere, but they were tinted just right so that no one from the street could see inside. It was bright out, and plenty of light came in—so much that Will didn't bother turning on any lights. He went over to the small desk in the corner. I knew there was a record player under there, and I stood there and waited patiently as he chose a record. It was whatever classical music they had been using during the ballet class, and I smiled at the sound of it as it came across the entire studio. Will pushed buttons, turning on more speakers until the whole downstairs shared the same sounds. He turned it up.

"Are we really dancing?" I asked, calling to him over the music.

He grinned at me as he headed back my way. "No," he said, calling back to me.

I stepped toward him and we fluidly converged in the middle of the studio space. Music was swirling all around us, and I went to him and he caught me. We twirled around in a dreamy motion. My body tingled where he touched me, which was everywhere. My body was against his, and he moved, swaying to the gentle slow rhythm of the music.

"Anne Rose."

"Yes?"

"I need you to close your eyes."

I didn't question him. I simply closed my eyes. I kept them closed, trusting Will, letting him hold me.

"Can you keep them closed?" he asked.

"Yes," I said.

"Will you?"

"Yes," I said easily.

I knew Will enough to know he wouldn't ask me to do anything bad, so it was a given that I'd do whatever he asked.

"Keep them closed and no peeking, okay?" he confirmed.

I nodded contently and I felt him move to where he was standing behind me. "I'm going to guide you somewhere," he said. "We're going to walk to a different room. I'm going toward the back, and I'll take you to a secret room that's hidden in a wall."

"Seriously?" I asked, smiling. Suddenly, keeping my eyes closed was much harder. I had to fight myself for a second.

"Hang on, hang on, stop," I said, pulling away from Will before we could go too far. I stared at him, blinking away the blurriness and focusing on his face. "Are you being serious?"

Will nodded. He was wearing an easy smile. There was soft lighting in the room, and music all around us, and he was talking about a secret room. It felt like a dream.

"I'm totally serious. It's one of the most beautiful little rooms you've ever seen in your life, and I want to take you there, but I can't show you the way. My sister was actually mad at me when I figured out where it was."

"Then why are you taking me there?" I asked smiling with wide eyes.

"She doesn't care if I go up there now, she was just mad at me for finding it." He smiled at my look of disapproval. "Would it make you feel better to know that I'm planning on telling her we were there?"

"Yes, but why wouldn't you just ask her ahead of time?"

"Because I didn't think about bringing you here until she had already left. Come on, I promise I'll tell her and she'll be fine with it. But you have to keep your eyes closed. I can't show you the way till we're married."

"Okay," I said, closing my eyes and loving the referral to our future wedding. "I promise, I won't peek. I don't even want to."

He moved when I closed my eyes, and the next thing I knew, he kissed me. I wasn't expecting it, but I kissed him back, smiling at the fact that I was still keeping my eyes closed. His mouth was warm and soft, and he kissed me several times, but I didn't open my eyes. I had no problem just closing them and enjoying the moment.

"Was that just a trick to get me to close my eyes, because I would have kissed you with my eyes open."

"No, I'm really taking you to a secret room. The kiss wasn't part of the plan. Now we're seriously going to start walking. Don't open your eyes." Will moved around me again, and I could feel when he started to guide me.

Chapter 19

Will stood behind me, leading me to the mysterious secret room. I kept my eyes closed, seeing nothing, only feeling and hearing him— smelling him. I was completely confused and wondered if the surprise was that there was something secret *in* a room and not an actual secret room.

I was aware that we were moving across open space, but I had no idea about my direction or speed. The music was all around me. Will was all around me. I had no desire to open my eyes. I didn't want to know where he was taking me. As far as I was concerned, knowing would have taken away from the magic of it all.

Without my vision, I found it was easy to fall into a loose state where I let Will completely lead me. I stepped where his body told me to step. He was behind me, supporting me and guiding me. I got butterflies at the vulnerable feeling of trusting him so fully. I leaned into him, smiling even though he probably couldn't see me.

"Okay, now we're headed into a room, but don't open your eyes yet." Will pulled me close to him, holding me. It felt as though we were squeezing into a small area and it sounded like he closed the door behind us.

"The music is still going," I said.

"Yeah, I clicked all of the buttons at the record stand, which includes the secret room."

I heard noises after the door closed—noises next to us that were louder than the music. Will had shifted in front of me, and he held me close. I stood there with my eyes closed, holding onto him, trusting him. There were the sounds of machine parts and moving metal and wood. I thought the floor might've moved under my feet, but it hadn't. It was just the noise in the wall. It got a little bit harder, at that point, to keep my eyes closed. I had a fight with myself, but I was able to do it.

Seconds later, Will said, "Okay, have you peeked?"

"No," I said with conviction, since I hadn't.

He held me by the shoulders. "All right, turn around and face this way. Take one step, and I'll put your hands on a rail. You will be at the bottom of a spiral staircase. It curves to the right. Take it slow. I'll be behind you, but you can go ahead and start climbing it. When you get five or six steps up, open your eyes."

I listened to Will and did as he said. Sure enough, he put my hands on a rail as soon as I took that first step forward. He was right behind me, leading me. I counted out loud, whispering, and smiling as I moved slowly with my eyes closed.

"One... two... three... four... five... six... are you sure I can open?" I asked, pausing with my eyes still closed.

"Yes, do it, open, look." I opened my eyes. I had my eyes so firmly closed that I had to blink to figure out how I was situated and what I was looking at. There was a gorgeous room with the sun beaming brightly down through a window in the ceiling. The room was full of wood in rich, amber tones.

The stairs were made of wood, and the room had a lot of it as well, the floors and the lower part of the walls. The rest of the walls were painted green, and as I stepped higher onto the staircase, I was able to see that two walls were lined with gorgeous book cases full of books and knickknacks.

There were plants hanging and some on shelves, and there was beautiful décor and furniture. In the corner was a huge chair, large enough for two people. In front of it was a table and two smaller chairs with a beautiful rich, jewel-toned oriental rug that tied the whole room together. I felt like I had been transported to a different time and place—a room-sized treasure box. It was cozy and beautiful and I had never seen anything like it.

I slowly made my way to the top of the steps, taking in everything I could. The experience was overwhelming. I took a few slow steps, coming to stand in the center of the room and look around. Will walked over and stood beside me, gently resting his hand on my back.

"Where the heck are we?" I asked stiffly, turning to look at him.

"We're in my sister's building, in a hidden room. Did you seriously not look that whole time?"

I smiled. "No, I didn't. My eyes were completely closed. We came up steps, so I know we're upstairs, but... how... where..."

Will walked to the right to a small half-circle table that was hugging the wall.

"This is another door," he said, gesturing to the table. "It leads to Tara and Trey's apartment."

I could tell by the way he was looking at me that he wanted me to go to him. I leaned into him, and he took me into his arms, holding me gently.

"Should we feel bad about being here?" I asked, standing next to him and speaking softly, flirting. The music was still playing up there, and it only added to the surreal feeling of it all.

"Do you feel bad right now?" he asked, staring at me, speaking softly, and flirting right back.

How could I possibly feel bad right now?

"No," I said. "But should we? Would Tara care?"

"She doesn't want me bringing anyone up here, but she also doesn't mind me using it. She said she was secretly glad I knew so that someone besides her and Trey could enjoy it. I think I'm the only one, though, unless she told our mom. That's one reason I have a key to the downstairs. I told her I wouldn't ever bring friends up here, but she knows I love you and I show you everything, so... it's fine."

I looked upward, staring at the ceiling, toward the window which was sending a direct beam of bright light into the room, causing it to glow. I noticed that the spiral stairs I had been climbing continued, leading upward to a hatch in the ceiling.

"Where do they lead?" I asked even though the obvious answer was the roof. At this point, with all the surprises, Will could say Mars, and I might believe him, "The roof," he said. "I have a key if you want to go out there."

"I think I'm good right here," I said. "As long as Tara doesn't mind."

"She doesn't," he promised me.

"Well, her secret's safe with me," I said. "I'm not even going to look when we leave. I'll keep my eyes closed and let you guide me out."

I kicked my shoes off and went for the gigantic chair in the corner of the room. I leaned against the corner of it, motioning to all the open space as I glanced at Will with a smile.

He knew I was inviting him, and he smiled. He took off his shoes and came toward me, wearing a mischievous half-grin that had me wanting to giggle. The sight of Will combined with the surreal nature of this room and the classical music made me feel like I was in a different dimension. He came toward me slowly.

There was some sort of promise in his expression. I had no idea what he was saying, but he was promising something. It was out of sheer delight and nervousness and not being able to wait for him, that I readjusted, flipping around and lying with my back on the seat of the chair. My legs were crossed at the ankles and sticking straight up in the air. The chair was so deep that I had to push forward a little to get my head to hang off the edge of it.

I saw Will again, only now he was upside-down. He was only a foot or two from me by the time I resituated where I was staring at him from my new perspective. He came closer, sitting on the floor in front of me where he was only a foot away, staring straight at me.

"You look different from upside-down," I said. "Your eyes are on the bottom."

He laughed. "Your eyes are on the bottom, too," he said staring at me.

I reached out and touched his jaw. "And your mouth is upside-down."

"No, my mouth is right side up, yours is upside-down."

I touched his cheek, staring thoughtfully at his upside-down mouth. With the way it was facing, the upper part had no indentation and the bottom part had one. It was not at all what I was used to with Will's lips, but it was handsome. I smiled at it when I was able to imagine his top lip for his bottom and vice versa.

"What are you laughing at?" he asked.

"I see your mouth upside-down," I said, smiling and staring at it.

He positioned himself next to me where he was leaning against the chair and hovering over my face. "What's it look like?" he said.

"You came so close, I thought you were going to kiss me just now." (I'd say just about anything to get him to do it.)

"I am going to kiss you," he said.

"When is it going to happen?" I whispered in a needy tone that caused him put his mouth closer. He leaned down and put his cheek to mine. He let his mouth graze my cheek but he didn't kiss me.

"When I say," he said, his mouth was so close to my cheek that it touched me when he spoke. The words combined with the feel of his mouth on my skin. I could not handle it.

"What if I wanted to be the one to say?" I said.

I was comfortable lying on my back. The chair was so large that there was plenty of room for me to sprawl out. Will stayed next to me, leaning over me and letting his face brush against mine. Sun streamed in through the skylight, but we were tucked in the shade. Music was playing, and I felt like I was in heaven.

"Say it, then," Will said.

I was so lost in thought that I had no idea what he was referring to. I made a face, and he smiled.

"You just told me you wanted to be the one to say when I kiss you, and I said you can. You can be the one to decide."

I pulled back to stare at him. "Now, then," I said.

"Now?" he asked, smiling.

I grinned at the sight of his upside-down smile, and then I leaned up and kissed it. It was a completely different experience, kissing Will upside-down—and yet it was exactly the same. I kissed him two or three more times before I pulled back.

"Hang on," I said, and I began to readjust. "Come on," I said, smiling and reaching out for him. Will stood up and swiveled over me, getting settled in the corner of the chair. I went to him, curling up beside him, looking out at the room and feeling like we were sitting in some sort of magic portal.

"This is the first time since we've known each other that we have no secrets at all." I cuddled next to Will, feeling thankful for his big masculine presence. "My family knows you, and your family knows me, and there's no fighting or hiding."

"You're right. This is the first time that I'm me and you're you and we can just be together without worrying about someone finding out."

I grinned at him. "As it stands now, I want *everyone* to find out."

"Just marry me then," he said.

"I will," I said. "I'd love to."

"When?" he asked. He absentmindedly ran his fingertips down my arm.

"On Valentine's Day," I said.

"When is that? Like eight or nine months?" he asked.

I counted on my fingers as I listed off months June, July, August, etc., all the way to February.

"Nine months," I said.

"Okay, so, that sounds like a plan to me," Will said.

I sat up a little bit, looking at him with a curious expression. "Were you being serious?" I asked.

"Weren't you?" he asked.

"Kind of. Mostly. I would marry you, but I didn't think you were actually asking so I just sort of made up Valentine's Day and all that."

"Oh, because I thought it was a good idea."

"You did?" I asked.

He smiled at me. "Yes."

"Valentine's Day?"

"Yeah, why not?"

"I don't even know what day of the week that is, but okay then, let's do it. Is that too soon?" I added, after I thought about it.

"No way," he said. "I was just thinking it might not be soon enough."

I leaned upward, smiling a little as I let my mouth touch his. Our lips stuck together in a soft, sticky kiss.

"Now you're not upside-down," he said.

I smiled. "I was just thinking that." I kissed him again. "I like you, Will Castro," I said, between gentle kisses. He grinned. "I like the man you are on the inside. And I like your face, and your hair and nose and your mouth."

"Thank you," he said with a slow amused grin. He kissed me again. "I like your insides, and your face and all that stuff, and your mouth, too. I *love* those things, actually," he added. "Come here, I need more of you."

Will got situated, pulling me up in his arms, positioning me closer to him. He was holding me, and I curled up with him. I put my hand on the side of his big face. My fingertips were near his eyes, and the tip of my thumb was near the corner of his mouth. I used it to trace the bottom edge of his lip.

Will proceeded to kiss me in a way he had never kissed me before. It started off soft and delicate and slowly built into something different, more passionate. In those moments, tucked in the corner of that secret room, I was tender and vulnerable with him and he was the same with me. And that was the way we both wanted it.

Chapter 20

Nine months later
Valentine's Day

Will and I both felt like dad-blasted Valentine's Day would never arrive. We were both so ready to get married that we almost eloped several times during the months that led up to it.

We had a lot going on, though.

I made the move from Houston to Galveston, and I got into a new routine that was pretty much the opposite of the one I had been maintaining previously. I now lived in Galveston and went to Houston about once a week, usually on Saturday, to have lunch with my family. Will and I now saw each other six days a week instead of one, and I knew that was how it should be. I had never been happier.

I was working at the restaurant Monday through Thursday. I went in early to prep and work on new dishes, and then I would stay and cook for lunch service. I was off work by three every day, and even after all that cooking at the restaurant, I still went home and made dinner for Will. He was easy to please and never turned down anything I cooked, but he had a few dishes that were his favorites, and I had worked them into a steady rotation. We ate with his parents sometimes, and also with the Elliots, Tara, or one of his cousins, but I cooked for him about four times a week, and it was something I loved to do.

Will had been putting a lot of time and effort in at the hardware store, and it was fun to watch them grow and expand. He was in a position where he checked on jobs and managed the managers.

The storefront had always been a staple in Galveston, but now they were growing, filling orders and taking jobs in other towns. It was a busy time for both of us. Individually, we were moving, working, growing, learning, and we'd meet up in the evenings feeling spent but happy and ready to tell each other about our day.

So, there was not even an ounce of doubt in my mind about this marriage—not even a speck of it. In fact, both Will and I felt like the day couldn't come soon enough.

I prepared myself for the big moment in a back bedroom at Daniel and Abby's house. My mom was in there with me, along with my friend Maggie from Houston. I had also gotten really close to Will's sister, Tara, and she had been in and out of the room while I was getting ready.

She had currently gone out to see how everything was going. I was nervous about this evening, terrified about all eyes being on me, but I couldn't wait to be Mrs. Castro.

Valentine's Day fell on a Friday, and our wedding was set to begin at 6pm with a reception and dinner to follow. The Elliots had catered it. My dad, Kyle Kennedy, was going to walk me down the aisle, and so was my dad, Michael Elliot. I would be escorted by two gentlemen, and everyone was fine with that. Michael and I had gotten to know each other better recently, and I felt like it was the right thing to do. Thankfully, my other dad didn't have feelings about it.

Michael still lived in Houston, but I had seen him at least a dozen times since that first encounter. I had taken to calling him *Pops*, and I now called Helen and Mike by *Nana* and *Grandy* which were the names they made up when Megan's kids were young.

It was thirty minutes till show time and my hair and makeup were done. All I had to do was put on my dress and veil. I was wearing a simple satin dress that was tight around the bodice but had a gorgeous full skirt that hit the floor, even with my heels on. My mother was the one who helped me zip it.

"Ooh, goodness, I shouldn't have had that slice of cake last night," I said, joking around when she pulled at the long zipper. She and Maggie both laughed at my comment, but then they stood back to look at me once I was in my dress.

"Oh, Anne Rose, it looks so amazing," Maggie said.

My mom blinked and stared upward just the right way that I knew she was trying to hold back tears. "You look beautiful," she said in that joyful-crying tone that proud mothers had.

I turned a little, regarding my reflection in the mirror. I was happy with how I looked in the dress, but honestly, this was all just a means to make me Will's wife. I was still standing there a few seconds later when Tara came back.

"Knock, knock," she said peeking her head in before she came inside. "Anne Rose, sister, goodness, you look so beautiful in that! Oh, my goodness, Will's gonna die. He's gonna cry."

"We're *all* going to cry," Maggie said.

"I'm already crying," my mom said.

"Hey, I was wondering if I could steal you for a minute," Tara said to me. "Can you walk out here into the hallway with me for just a minute?"

"Sure, what's up?" I asked.

"My brother."

"No way, José!" my mom said.

"Yeah, he can't see her before the—"

"He's not going to look at her," Tara assured them. "He just wants to tell her something." She reached out and took a hold of my hand. She was a protective older sister, and if Will wanted to talk to me, Tara was going to be sure he got his wish.

"Of course," I said easily, and Tara began leading me to the door.

She turned to me as we walked into the hallway. "He's right out here, but he's got his eyes closed."

I caught a quick glimpse of Will standing there in his black suit. He was so handsome and sharp that my heart leapt. I let out a little gasp and quickly closed my eyes.

"Am I supposed to keep my eyes closed, too?" I asked, holding onto Tara.

"No, no, unless you want to, but no, there's no rule about the bride doing that."

I didn't know where Tara had gotten her information, but it sounded right. I believed her. I opened my eyes instantly, staring straight at the love of my life from only a few feet away. He was standing there, holding a gift that was in a box and wrapped with a bow on it.

"He's going to make me cry," I warned, looking at Tara.

"Don't cry," Will said.

"I love you," I replied, unable to contain myself.

He smiled with his eyes closed, and my heart felt like it might explode.

"Where are you?" he asked. But I was already reaching for him. I touched Will's arm, and he grabbed me with his free hand. "I love you, too," he said. "I'm so pumped."

"Look, you two, I'm headed back out there to help Uncle Daniel and Evan get everybody seated. When y'all are done, you know what to do. Just keep your eyes closed while she gets back in the room."

"Yes, ma'am," Will said, teasing his sister.

"Seriously, Will, no peeking," she said.

"I won't," he promised, smiling.

Tara retreated down the hall, but before she rounded the corner, she smiled at me. "You look beautiful, Anne Rose," she said. "Oops, sorry, I shouldn't tempt my brother. No peeking. Nothing to see here. She looks really... normal. Totally normal."

Tara rounded the corner, leaving me in the hallway, staring at my future husband. His suit fit his big athletic body like it was custom made for him, and I almost cried at how handsome he was.

"I want to give you this to take in there and open," he said. "I knew you had a few minutes before you come out."

He pushed the box toward me. It was long and narrow. "Is it a mini keyboard?" I guessed, being playful and saying the first thing that came to my mind.

"No. It's actually something I made. Just know when you open it that I made it for you. By hand. I had to take lessons. A bunch of lessons. It takes practice. I had a little help with this one because I wanted to get it perfect, but I did most of it myself."

"What is it?" I asked.

"I'm not telling you," he said smiling.

"When would you have time for lessons?"

"Saturdays. When you go to Houston."

He pushed the box toward me again. "Take it and set it down for a second. You can open it when I walk away."

I did as he said. I took the wrapped gift from him and turned to set it down. Quickly, I went to Will again, taking a hold of his hands since he had no idea where I was or what I was doing.

"Anne Rose, it is almost impossible to keep my eyes closed. I have no idea how you do it when we go up to Tara's room. I'm not going to look, but I'm *really* fighting the urge right now."

"Yeah, but I don't want to see where that room is. That's part of the mystery of it for me. I'll probably keep my eyes closed to go up there, even after we get married."

I was holding his hands, but he reached up like he was searching for my face. I placed his palm on the side of my cheek. He leaned toward me and breathed in through his nose. "I can feel you and I can smell you."

We were so close.

"You can kiss me too," I said, feeling like I might burst if he didn't. Will and I had spent a lot of time together. We had been in love for over a year. We had waited to be intimate physically, and in that regard, it felt like this day might never arrive.

"Can I? May I?" he asked.

"You can and you may," I said.

"Is that not violating some kind of rule?" he asked.

"No," I said. "I've never, *ever*, heard a rule against kissing with your eyes closed before the wedding."

"Kiss me, then," he said.

I leaned in and placed my lips on Will's, and he wrapped his hands around me, pulling me closer by the waist. He kissed me several times, gentle, patient, forbidden, pre-wedding kisses that made my toes curl. I pulled back, feeling like I might get too carried away if I didn't break the contact.

I leaned in next to his ear and whispered, "I love you the most a girl ever loved a boy, Will Castro."

He smiled. "You have to get back in that room right now, or else I'm going to open my eyes and look at you."

"Don't do it," I said with a smile in my voice. I gave his hand a squeeze. "Keep your eyes closed. I'm going to pick up my box and then go back in the room. I'll yell at you once it's all clear."

"Okay," he said.

I kissed his cheek. "You're the finest looking man I have ever seen in my life," I said. I moved to turn and pick up the box. "I can't wait to be your wife." I added in a rushed tone as I made it to the door.

"I can't wait for that, either," he said.

"Give me like five more seconds," I said, making sure all my skirts were inside before I closed the door.

"I'm opening!" he announced after the five seconds were up.

"Go ahead," I said, through a crack in the door. "See you in a minute," I added, closing it.

"What was that all about?" my mom asked.

I held the box to my chest and sighed. "I'm in love," I said.

Maggie laughed, and my mom came toward me. "What is it?" she asked, inspecting the box.

"I don't know. Will said he made it."

"I can't believe you talked to Will," Maggie said as I began to open the box.

"He kept his eyes closed," I assured her. "He said he wanted to give me this."

"He made it?" Mom asked, looking on curiously as I opened it.

It was a wooden box. I knew it was the workmanship of a man named Donnie who had been friends with their family for years. Tara's husband, Trey, had been working a little with him, and my first thought was that Will had gotten into woodworking with Mister Donnie.

It was a beautiful box. But then I opened it, and I realized that the box wasn't the gift. I blinked. I couldn't believe it.

"What is it?" my mom asked impatiently.

"A knife."

"A knife?" they both said at the same time.

"A chef's knife," I said. I took it out of the box, holding it, testing the weight of it in my hand. Will could have bought me any number of things as a wedding gift, but none could ever be as special as this.

"He made that?" my mom asked.

"Yes," I said.

"How?" Maggie asked. "How do you make a knife?"

"I have no idea," I said, turning it over in my hand. "But he did it." I tested the sharpness of the edge with my thumb before balancing it in my hand again. "And it's a nice one," I said. "I can't wait to use this."

"Of all the gifts a groom could give to his bride on his wedding day," my mom said, shaking her head. "My son-in-law makes a knife." She stared at me with a proud smile. "But the most important thing is that he makes my daughter happy."

I nodded thoughtfully, considering Will and the night we had to look forward to. And I knew my mother was correct. Happiness was important, and Will Castro was the person who made me feel that way.

Epilogue

A year later

Will and I bought and moved into our first home a week ago, and we were still getting settled in it. I enjoyed decorating, and I looked forward to seeing if Will noticed the things I had changed and rearranged every day when he got home from work.

His mother gave us one of her paintings as a wedding gift, and I loved it so much that I had built our living room's color scheme around it. It was a grand piece, five feet wide by four feet deep. I felt at home when I stood in my new living room and looked at it.

Nana and Grandy had given us a gift card to Sears and our new television was delivered today. I had just finished setting it up and arranging some things on the entertainment center before I turned to look at the painting. I was staring at it when Will came in.

"Hey," I said. I had heard him open the door, and I turned to look that way when he came inside.

"Hey," he said. "It smells great in here." I went to him, hugging him and leaning up for a kiss. His mouth tasted like sweat, which didn't surprise me because he had gone to his dad's gym for two hours after work.

"I didn't take a shower yet," he said, even though I didn't care. His hair was damp with sweat, and to be honest, it was really attractive.

"What's for dinner?" he asked. "It smells really good."

"I tried that shrimp and asparagus soup again. I puréed everything this time, so it's real smooth. And I have some roast beef from the restaurant and some bread that I'm going to toast with seasoning and olive oil."

"I can't wait," he said. He kissed my neck.

"Also, our new TV came in," I said.

He looked that way, but only for a second before kissing me again this time on the cheek. He smelled musky in the best way possible. It was a mix of deodorant and sweat, and I loved it. Obviously, I loved everything about this man.

I had told him to look at the TV in hopes that he would notice the box on the entertainment center, but he didn't. He barely even looked that way before kissing me again. "Looks great, thank you," he said.

"I made you something," I said.

"You make me lots of things," he replied. "And that soup is number one on my list right now. It smells sooo good."

"No, I mean I made you something that's not food," I said.

"What is it?" he asked. He paused and looked around the room.

"It's in that box," I said. I pointed to the wooden box.

It was the very same box that my knife had come in, so Will instantly looked at me and said, "You made a knife? When did you..." He had still been doing blacksmithing every other weekend or so, and he looked at me with a curious expression like he was trying to figure out when I could have possibly taken lessons.

I grinned at his confusion. "It's not a knife," I said. "But I did have to take lessons. A few."

"What lessons?" he asked.

"Sewing."

"Sewing?"

I nodded. "Helen's friend, Joan. She's teaching me. I was thinking I'd get a machine and put it in that extra bedroom, but I didn't want to buy one until I gave you your surprise."

He was smiling as he crossed the room to retrieve the box.

"Is it a scarf?" he asked.

"A scarf?" I said. "When do you ever wear a scarf?"

"I don't, but I was trying to think about what you could sew that would fit in this box."

"Just open it and find out," I said.

Will opened the box, and then he took out the colorful fabric that was inside. He set down the box and looked at me with a curious, confused expression as he unfolded it. "It looks like a baby doll shirt," he said.

"It is a baby doll shirt," I said, smiling at him. "Without the doll."

"A baby shirt? Why'd you sew a baby shirt?"

My smile broadened. "Why do you think?" I asked.

"Is it for a baby?" he asked.

His expression was so intense that I had to laugh. "Yes, it's for a baby," I said.

"*My baby?*" he asked.

I nodded, and he dropped the outfit on to the nearest surface before rushing to me and taking me into his arms.

I laughed some more at the sudden reaction, and Will held me tight, staring straight into my eyes and breathing heavily from the split-second effort to rush to me.

"Is my baby in here?" he asked, referring to my body.

I laughed as I nodded.

"Are you serious? Are you sure?"

I nodded again. "I went to the doctor and everything."

"What'd they say? How's it doing? How's it doing in there?"

"Fine," I said. "Everything's good. He said we're due in October."

"October? Really? Good. That's amazing. (He kissed me.) I'm so happy. I'm so excited. I can't wait. We have to tell everybody. How are you? How are you feeling? Do you need any special food or anything? Pickles? I think my mom needed salsa."

Will was kissing me between all of his questions, and I had to laugh at his enthusiasm. "I'll make sure I'm getting all my vitamins," I said. I looked at him, straight into his dark brown, faceted eyes. "And as for how I'm feeling... (I smiled.) I'm feeling wonderful."

The End
(till book 7)

Thanks to my team ~ Chris, Coda, Jan, and Glenda

Made in the USA
Middletown, DE
20 November 2021

53025396R00123